Today's HorroRscope

Stuart McCusker

Not a smidge of what follows is true........ except that the New York Mets are America's team (at least in my opinion). The rest is all fiction, and I hope you like it.

"no real names or persons, other than Rusty the dog, who graciously allowed me to use his name for the bargain price of a few cheeseburgers, were used in this book. Anything close to anything or anyone real is unintended, and a coincidence."

Stuart McCusker

CONTENTS

Paul,
To a great neighbor + even greater friend; I hope all your horoscopes are good), and your dreams come true!

Your Friend
Stuart McWester

P.S. Rusty misses you

THANK YOU

This book could not have been completed without help from the following people. If you don't like it please note, the people below had a hand in it too.

To my parents – Thank you for always believing; and for that first T-bird you gave me.

To my children Jake and Melanie – your shenanigans keep me young. Thank you for everything; it's the best part of my life. Keep it up.

To my brothers Fred McCusker, John McCusker, Jeffrey McCusker, Jimmy McCusker, and sister Helaine Krob, (who also wrote a great book called *The Road Rises Up*). Thank you for all your help, love, and support over the years.

To my friends – I don't have the space to give it the right words for your support, ("You wrote a book? You did? We were stunned that you could read one, nevertheless write one!"). Such touching support still brings a tear to my eye, and I find it hard to put it in words. Good friendships are priceless. With that being said, let's get a bit more priceless.

To the 3 Detroit Divas: Kellie Harvey Biddle, Sue Jiminez Artinian, and Lana Mazur. Kellie, my partner in crime on this, reading several drafts; your help was enormous, and I will never be able to repay you. Perhaps I'll let you win when you race your Charger against my Thunderbird (powered by the famous Ford Thunderjet motor). I will give you a much-needed head start. And Sue and Lana, you Divas have been dynamite as well, with your fantastic help; Washington D.C. is still recovering from your visit. Come back.

To Michelle Martin – for patiently listening for years about this debacle, always encouraging me to write it, and helping me finish it.

To Willy B. – From one gambler to another, thank you for all your tips on how to invest and make cash. Or rather make it disappear; I don't know how I can ever repay you. Or anyone else.

To my friends Ronnie Braxton, Mike Covington, and Ken Tully. Thanks for always being there.

To my favorite 3 writers; (please buy their books) – Your encouragement and advice was huge and will never be forgotten. Thank you for showing me the way.

Helaine Krob – my sister, and author of *The Road Rises Up*; Thank you for all the encouragement through the years. Since this is published, I promise to now return your book *On Writing* (*How to Write a Book*). I know it's overdue and will pay any late fees. Thank you.

Eric Michlowitz – author of *The Mystics' Treachery* - "Stuart, 500 words a weekend, you can do it!" (great, great, advice). Just remember, the Yankees aren't all that Amazing; the Mets (my team) are, and it's never too late to come home. Thank you for all.

Ralph Peluso – author of *512*; (Another notorious Yankees fan). You too please remember the Yankees lose once in a while, and the Mets are on the rise. And Tom Seaver is still the greatest right hander the game has ever had. Thank you for all throughout the years.

To my editor Andrew H. Sullivan – Your advice and help was outstanding, and I will be eternally grateful and look forward to the next ones.

To my graphics and logistics team – Andrew Donaldson (Logistics and also some editing), Rachel Toney, and Thomas Smak of MaudlinDigital.com for the cover art. Thank you guys for great work; I look forward to the next ones with you as well.

To Jason White, the newest editor to the team, you have a great future editing, thank you and keep it up!

To the World's Most Dangerous Posse, whose friendship I will be eternally grateful for, despite all the errors several of you have made in baseball and softball over the years. Jim Koshuta, Jim Lavey, Brad Camp, and Richard Darcy. Thanks for all the shenanigans over the years, and the feedback on this book; I appreciate it all.

And last but not least:

To Tres Juevos, the greatest softball player I ever saw (I will not use your real name since you're shy and reserved); I never saw a guy hit three home runs in one inning till you did it.

THE PROLOGUE

Good God was that loud! The 600-pound telco cabinet swung around and slammed into the side of the Statue of Liberty and resounded like an enormous gong. And if the noise wasn't enough, sitting fourteen stories up in the statue, the impact shook the statue as if it was about to fall down. If that doesn't get you excited, call your doctor, or, better yet, have a friend call one because you're in a coma. You're not seeing things right. The Statue of Liberty is in danger and I was in the torch.

"Cam, are you able to stabilize it at all?" I barked into the headset.

"I don't know, Billy, but hang on tight. It's swinging around and gonna hit again!! Hold on!"

GOOOOONNGGG!!!!

Between the noise and the entire structure shuddering, I was going to pass out. Or die. Or have to pay for this mess for the rest of my life. This was the fourth time it hit, and each time it was louder and more violent. Are those dummies *trying* to knock the statue down? Maybe somehow the spinning cabinet was picking up momentum. Regardless, this was not how our installation of telco gear was supposed to go . . . And something good needed to happen soon—before we knocked it down with me and the tech guys inside Lady Liberty.

We were in perhaps the most iconic of the American monuments, installing a highly technical piece of cell phone equipment in the torch of the Statue of Liberty, and one of the cables stabilizing the cabinet had broken, causing the cabinet to swing unrestrictedly around the statue and slam into it. Also, due to the hollowness, the acoustics were

1

so loud that Pete Townsend and the Who would be proud to claim it. Unfortunately for me, this was not a concert, and the vibrations were not the result of an electric guitar melting faces. No, this big ol' lady felt like she was going to topple over. And, dear reader, the worst part about all of this—worse than the ear-shattering noise or the prospect of being crushed by a giant as if I were a Lilliputian—was that I *knew* something like this could happen. I was to blame, you might say. Or, my bad "luck", we'll call it.

"Cam! What are you seeing up there?" I screamed into the headset, watching the New York City skyline rock back and forth.

"Billy, hold on to something. It's swinging by and about to hit near the head!"

No shit. I was already gripping Lady Liberty so hard I was at risk for an assault charge. "Cool! I can't wait!" Nothing left to do but meet tragedy with humor.

GOOOOONNNNNGGGG!!!!

I lost my balance when the cabinet struck the statue in the back of the head, and I rocked and rolled on the floor as the great woman shuddered and shook. As I jostled around, damn near over the rail of the torch, trying to keep my head from getting whacked, I was wondering how I could have possibly gotten into this. I was normally not a risk taker—I had a good job with a telecom installation company and kept to my routine with some music shows and an occasional rowdy night out with friends, but this was more than I could handle, and that last hit shook this thing hard. I didn't know how many more it could take.

I believe, I believe, I believe, I was saying to myself, over and over, a mantra prepping myself for the inevitability of collapse, the statue being like 150 years old, or whatever it was.

If I could go back in time a week, I'd certainly do some things differently. Never in my wildest dreams did I think a few stupid comments could lead to something like this, but apparently, it could. And let the record state, before the events of the last week happened to me, *no way* would I have believed this was even possible. I was a skeptic extraordinaire. But, dear reader, sorry to bring you into this again, I need you to consider the following as a favor to me: please, please, please, watch what you say about things you don't know for certain, and be wary of that old adage, "Be careful what you wish for, you might just get it." I didn't get *it*, and boy, did I ever *get* it—if you know what I mean.

I must have bumped my head or went inside myself to protect from the chaos. All I was able to think about was how it all started innocently enough, last Friday afternoon, a quaint and typical (if but slightly warmer than average) April in the year 2016. I was planning a happy hour get together with my best friend Mike and three lovely ladies. It was the twenty-third of April, to be exact, which seemed like an important detail to iron out in case this was my last few moments on Earth. Little had I known it would lead to the most chaotic week of my life and—*GOOOONNNNNG*!!!! (there goes Lady Liberty again)— apparently testing everything I ever believed in, including my notion that I'd live to see old age. If only I hadn't taken that dare…

***

FRIDAY
Happy Hour

"Outstanding!"

I'd just got off the phone with my idiot wingman Mike, and we now had a Friday night happy hour with three very attractive ladies teed up. "What time and where? And who, again?"

Mike was ecstatic in his reply. "Well, we got Jackie, Sue, and Maureen. And word is that Maureen just canned her boyfriend, so even *you* may have a chance. We're going to the Crazy Horse in DC, and there's going to be a Stones cover band there, so all of this should be great. Don't mess it up by plan enhancing, like you always do. We need to get there by six PM, so finish up whatever debacle you're involved in at work. We can't be late."

"Plan enhancing" is what we called anything that a well-meaning person tries to do to alter an already set up deal. *Do not* plan enhance; just show up and keep the wheels rolling. Mike, in fact, was a notorious plan enhancer himself, an irony which was lost on him, though not on me.

While I was grumbling about the pre-scold, I was thinking his plan sounded awesome. The girls were attractive, smart, and, above all, fun. Now, I, myself, did not look like Hollywood material. I worked at a telecom company and managed with people mostly on my sense of humor, which got me lucky from time to time. However, my claim to fame was that I was an outstanding softball player and know everything about baseball. In fact, I (and my posse would have no doubt confirmed this) am a genius at baseball. I'd been accused of knowing too much, and probably should get a life—this I simply wrote off as jealousy.

Damn Mike had me self-assessing as we got off the phone. I was thinking how I needed to finish some work and get out of here by five to get to DC by six. Normally I would have fired up my Mustang for that mission, but instead, I decided to take the Metro to the city so I didn't have to worry about driving in traffic all the way to Washington, D.C.

All I needed to do was give a quick update to my boss, and then I could bolt.

I shot an e-mail to my boss updating him on our projects for next week—big things happening, and I was a major player—and packed my work area so I could take off right after I heard back.

"Greg, I updated the cell site status report and posted it to the shared drive; one thing to note is two sites in Cincinnati have zoning issues and need legal to get involved. I note all of this in the comments column for each and believe it's not in a bad spot. Rhonda from legal is already engaged, so we're good."

He quickly responded, so I knew I was set to go.

"Thanks Billy. I saw it and we're good; I see you're packing up, so have a great weekend. Oh, remember next week we have that All Hands call, so we may or may not have to give some statuses to the group. But no worries if we do, I'll handle the PR and report creations. I may just need you to give me some details. Have a great weekend and we'll talk Monday."

One thing about my boss, Greg; he was a great guy. I'd worked with him at a few different companies. We were a good team and whenever a company hired him away, he brought his people with him. As anyone who works in telecommunications can attest, a more volatile industry does not exist. Telco companies are constantly buying, selling, bankrupting, or mismanaging themselves into vapor, so it's extremely ironic that the bestselling contraptions in the industry, used by untold millions, are called "smart phones." The word "smart" and this industry rarely occupy the same space; there must be a marketing genius out there that came up with it, though I had yet to meet that person. But my boss got it; we were all just trying to make a living and have some fun along the way.

Anyway, I was done with my week and needed to get out of there.

Reston, Virginia, was a great place to work and live, until you needed to be somewhere quick. It was caravan central around those parts in the afternoon, and, while I may have been a baseball genius, on occasion I got to talking and making myself late—which I could not do today, since this was a date. *Time to bolt. I can't be derailed due to traffic.*

Mike would have said it was a debacle and I should keep my mouth shut about baseball. Turning down Reston Parkway already garbled by traffic, I was beginning to think Mike was right and getting worried about making a bad impression . . . *If I'm not on a train by 5:30, I'm gonna be late.* The Metro was notoriously slow and had delays during rush hours, and if I wasn't on the 5:30 train, I was for sure going to miss intros, which was not the first impression I wanted to make.

Mike was already texting me for ETAs and status updates. *One day (hopefully soon) I am going to enjoy knocking him out, that ball buster.* At a red light, I shot him a quick reply: "On time, quit f-ing with me."

The light flared green and I burst out of the gate, winning a race no one else was having. I still felt great hitting 65 mph in 3.4 seconds and beating the next orange light, and the next and all along I was reciting my new thinking: *I'm going to be on time . . . these girls are not easy to schedule with . . . I'm not going to mess this up.*

Whether it was my chanting, or the rocket ship disguised as a car, I cut off four lights at two to three minutes per light and so turned a delay into a surplus of time. Once parked, getting onto the trains was the easiest part; I didn't care if I got a seat or not. I was reciting my new mantra (*I'm not going to mess this up . . .*) and added in another to keep myself calm in the most claustrophobic train I'd ever seen . . . *Just squeeze in and go.* And I did. It was 5:25, and the ride was about twenty-five minutes, so my timeline was still intact. Crazy Horse, the venue, was only a ten-minute walk from the M Street exit, so I would be there before the ladies, by my calculations. Everything was going to be all good.

Thank God! The Metro conductor must have been a born-again NASCAR racer; we hauled ass and I had factored in at least a few delays. *Must be my lucky day for once.* I'd been accused (unjustly so) of being a bad time manager and late to stuff (or maybe justly so, but I always made up for it by buying drinks). Anyway, I was making good time and dodging pedestrians like a pro on my way to Crazy Horse in ten minutes.

The Crazy Horse was a great place with a ton of history. It was just off M Street in Georgetown, and it had been there forever. It was near the older buildings and the waterfront, and just a really cool two-floor venue. The food was actually not bad for a bar. The second floor had an open view to the first, so you could sit up there, eat, and watch whatever band and not be in the masses.

If you wanted to get into the mix of dancing and seeing the band, you could head to the first floor, grab a table, or do the standing thing. On the way up, James Brown played there, and some other acts that hit it big, too. Billy Idol when he was with Generation X, and, believe it or not, The Blues Brothers. I heard the Stones held a small rehearsal there when their tour came through DC in the 70s. All in all, it was one of my favorite spots. Typically, it booked local bands, travelling up-and-comers, or some extremely cool tribute bands. Like, tonight's band, Tumbling Dice, was a well-traveled Rolling Stones cover band. So, I had a great feeling the night would be fun.

Our plan was to meet the girls at six, grab a table upstairs for drinks and food, then see how things went from there. I was fired up for, yes, some happy hour fun, but mainly for the band. The real Stones toured once a decade, and the tickets were crazy expensive. I figured, with a few drinks, and the loud sound (a Crazy Horse staple), with any luck, I'd feel like I was at a great Stones show in a small venue. On top of all this, I'm nearsighted, so it wasn't like they needed to look exactly like the actual guys.

As I crossed the M street bridge which officially delivered me into Georgetown, I knew I couldn't forget about the girls. Mike was always telling me to stay focused and don't let all the peripheral stuff we do get in the way of meeting someone. And it's true, I got bogged down with the details of the show and the food and mechanics of the evening and then, according to Mike—but I had to admit there was some truth to this—I talked the girls to death with trivia or ignored them in favor of the music. It had been a while…a long while in terms of the dating situation. And Mike was always on the prowl, so I had to remind myself to stay focused and be fun. Easier said than done.

So, I rolled up at a timely 6:05 and Mike was there, but the girls were not.

"They're running late, let's get upstairs, get a good table and some beers."

Mike was focused as shit. Didn't even bother with our normal handshake routine.

"Ok, sounds good, let's go."

I was happy to have some time to chat with Mike and game-plan a little before the girls arrived. I had a few questions for him and wanted to make sure I knew who was single and who wasn't and any past stories or triggers I should avoid…also, any sports affiliations I should go easy on.

Usually when I'm pressed for being somewhere on time it's a pain, but in this instance, he was right—by hauling ass down there, we got a great table upstairs, with a great view of the stage. *And* near the kitchen. Bonuses all around. We wouldn't wait years for drinks, and we could see the band. *The Crazy Horse really knows how to do it. If only I was old enough to have seen the Blues Brothers when they toured!* I supposed the fake Stones would have to do.

Anyway, Mike and I had a few minutes, so we jumped into our thing.

"You said that Maureen torpedoed Tommy? Really? I liked that dude. What's the deal?"

"Busted with a girl from his co-ed softball team. That dummy blew it, because Maureen's nice, too. Mo' said she wasn't too serious with him, but once she found out, he got torpedoed and sent packing."

Tommy was another friend who was not somebody I hung out with a lot, but he wasn't the devil either. Case in point, I once saw him get involved in a fight when some big drunk was pummeling a much smaller guy—Tommy got in the middle of it and broke it up. Saved that little guy's ass and didn't even know him. It's not cool for people to cheat on each other, but they were only dating for a few months. I didn't know how serious things were—sounded like not so much on either side—still, it wasn't cool.

"Is she doing ok? How'd he get caught?"

"Yeah, she's a strong one. No worries there, though you know it always sucks to be in that position. And somebody posted a pic on Facebook catching him in a lie. He was supposedly sick, and the dumbass ends up in a picture at a Redskins game. With Cindy. The other girl. Done."

"Oh. Gotta love Facebook. Hopefully Mo's not too broken up; I actually always thought she was pretty and nice, too."

"She's not too upset. I think she was going to end it anyway. At least, that's what she told me."

We chatted and caught up about work and other things. Mike was telling me about his dating exploits, which were hilarious and cringeworthy at times. Nothing from the girls for an hour, and I was beginning to think we'd been stood up. But then, 7:20, a text came through to Mike: "We're here, where are you guys?"

"Second floor, on the edge table by the orange and blue band posters."

"Ok cool, we'll be there in a second."

Up the stairs they came, and yes, it was worth the wait; all three of the girls looked great. We've known Maureen since high school, so tardiness, we knew, was one of her things, but it's not like this was a blind date. This was just a night for some fun; nothing heavy, so, we'd see where things went. Man, this plan was looking good.

Jackie, Sue, and Maureen arrived upstairs at our table and I got a bit nervous. I immediately thought of how great this was going. *Note to self: don't get too drunk.*

"Hi Mike, Hi Billy. These are my friends Jackie & Sue. They went to school with me at VCU in Richmond and are so glad we came to this place. I saw this band in Richmond, and they are so much like the Stones it's scary."

Maureen was upbeat, despite the breakup. She was always very positive, and I was glad she still had that joy that we'd come to know her for.

We all agreed how cool it was to not have to pay a ton of money to see the real Stones when we could just relax and see "the fake Stones" and still get to see a good show.

After a quick five minutes of introductions, we ordered some wings and nachos and had the usual get-to-know-each other small talk. I had to admit I was impressed; not only were Maureen's friends really attractive, they were really smart. Jackie had graduated with honors and was working on a Masters in international studies, and Sue apparently wrecked the school grading curves, graduating magna cum laude from VCU (I did not, hence me needing them to define it to me; 3.8 GPA or above for those keeping score), and was prepping for LSATs to try to get into Georgetown Law School.

How in the world Mike and I were at this table was a bit of a mystery. I was not a super smart student, and neither was he. However, Mike was in sales, which, I'm sure that had something to do with our luck, and I was glad to be the beneficiary of his talking game. Regardless, I didn't care how we got there. The looks from the patrons all around us confirmed my impression; these girls looked great and were getting a lot of attention. *Ok, Billy, enough facts and assessing. Time to make an impression...*

"What time does the show start?" asked Jackie.

"It's supposed to start around 7:30 and run two hours; a friend of mine saw them here a year ago," I chimed.

"Excellent. We have some time till it gets really loud," Mike said.

"Let's get some drinks and order our dinner before the show gets going. Despite this place being a bar, the food's pretty good. They have some fancy things, but the burgers and sandwiches are awesome. If anyone wants, we can get some wine."

We placed our orders, the girls getting chicken alfredo pasta, scallops, and a sandwich, and Mike ordering his usual burger; I ordered steamed shrimp. For drinks, a couple of glasses of wine, two fancy beers (none of which I knew), and Mike, I know, ordered a beer he had no idea what it was, and I ordered a bottle of Bud. Mike saw the girls were getting microbrew beers so he wanted to impress them. Meanwhile, I got a standard cheap one and Mike was pretending he was a connoisseur, part of his "game."

We had about an hour till the show and had a really great chat about the fate of the Washington Redskins (no playoffs, again), and what we thought the Nationals would do; I was and have always been a huge New York Mets fan, so, even though I played nice for Mo and the girls, I was actually hoping the Nats had a horrible season.   Though I was holding back, Mo remembered I was a Mets fan and that started a pretty active discussion on why the Mets suck, and that the planets were aligned for the Nats to have a great season. Mike wholeheartedly agreed and promptly told the table, "Even a voodoo spell couldn't stop the Nats; Max Scherzer just won the Cy Young award, and the Mets spend more time on the DL than at the ballpark." It was funny and true to a point.

It wasn't easy to dispute that, however, I did (they *are* my team) with: "Well, since we're talking 'voodoo', maybe somebody can put a spell on the Nats to finally win in the postseason, since they never have in their history. The Cubs supposedly got all kinds of guys to reverse their curse—the Red Sox, too. The Nats could use something to fix their horrific mojo. Being a Mets fan, I am so glad they suck when it counts, and even a team of witch doctors couldn't fix the Nats. Even if that stuff was real, which none of it is." (At the time of this debacle, the Nationals had never won a single playoff game; of course they did in

2019. This tale takes place before that event).

Well, apparently, I must have struck a raw nerve; all three girls, and Mike (I knew he was) were all huge Nats fans, and immediately got fired up. I heard about MVPs, Cy Youngs (Scherzer), arm surgeries (every Met starting pitcher). Jesus, I knew they were smart, but these were the type of attacks I expected from my wingman & softball buddies. They were kicking my ass and I like to think I'm a baseball genius, not a baseball punching bag. But I had to admit, it was a good fun conversation, especially when the voodoo thing and witch doctors came back into it.

"If there's any team out there that needs some witch doctors, it's the crappy Mets," Susie countered. "They should see if they can get a séance, sprinkle some pixie dust, or make a deal with the Devil to make it through a season. They suck. By the way, I have a friend who heard some major league players actually get their palms read to see what kind of season they should expect to have. I bet it was the Mets."

"No way do these guys do that stuff, and especially my team!"

I have to admit, however, professional athletes are some of the most superstitious people on the planet. Wade Boggs of the Red Sox, a Hall of Famer and a great, great hitter, used to eat nothing but chicken on game days, supposedly the same thing, at the same time, for like seventeen years. Other guys had rituals, too. Michael Jordan as a pro, for example, wore his North Carolina shorts under his Bulls uniform his entire career. This rumor about the Mets doing palm readings may actually have been true.

"Well? Does your team do this stuff or not? And if you're such a genius on baseball, do you think it's even possible? Palm readings? Care to bet on any of this?" Mike immediately went into "agree mode." It was a tactic I've seen him use before; agreeing with *anything* any girl he's chasing says. I was stunned by this betrayal this early in the night, however, though I should have known better.

Maybe the margaritas (on the rocks, no salt, by the way) were talking, but all I could get out was: "Palm readings and all this superstitious junk are the biggest bunch of bull! I welcome any and all bets; but unless you know a witch doctor, good luck trying to get this bet going, much less collect."

If only I knew then, what I know now all too well…

"Well, there's a palm reading place right down the street from here. Madame Pearl's House of Magic." This from Susie, helpfully leading

11

the charge. Apparently, I'd offended a future attorney, which was never a good idea.

"Since all of this stuff is fake and mumbo jumbo, I say you're too chicken to get your palm read! Let's all go right after the show! Maybe we should skip it!"

That last part brought on a very loud "NO!" from Maureen, who apparently had a thing for Mick Jagger—even a fake Mick Jagger.

"We're not missing the show under any circumstances."

I had to admit, I have a flaw (probably one of many, but one confirmed) in my own character; I have a very hard time turning down bets or dares, especially on baseball, the Mets, or something kooky like palm readings. Mike, of course, didn't believe any of this BS either, but these girls could have brought Area 51 and aliens into the discussion and he'd agree aliens are in Arizona or New Mexico, or wherever that crash allegedly happened. A wingman on a mission. My dumb ass just got pummeled into this bet.

"Fine. Sounds good. I say we all go, and Madame What's-her-name can even throw a Ouija board at me; none of this stuff is real. Let's go right after the 'Fake Stones' finish their set. I will bet anyone anything none of this stuff is real. I almost feel bad I'm gonna be taking your money. Almost."

By that time, our dinner and drinks had arrived. And even our waitress named Marissa had something to add. Being a former waiter, I knew you can't help but overhear stuff. Our conversation was a bit nuts, but she apparently wanted in on it, too.

"I've been to Madame Pearl's, and her readings are true. My friend Betty went there, and she totally read what was going on with her life: her deadbeat boyfriend, how her rent was going to go up, how we were going to have to work extra shifts here. It all came true. You guys should go, and you (looking directly at me) better watch it. She can spot a 'non-believer' a mile away and doesn't like them."

"Ooooooooh nooooo. I think I'll survive," I sarcastically chirped.

This night had turned into much more than I thought and was actually fun: some good (not mean) trash talking, three girls who knew sports really well (always a plus), the fake Stones soon (guaranteed to be fantastic), and a bet. Man, I was thinking to myself: *If any of them has a bad ass car, we'd be in trifecta territory.*

My wingman, despite his "agree mode," had put a great night together.

We finished our food just as "Start Me Up" began, and I was fired up. These Stones, fake or not, were rocking, and I was having a blast. From our vantage point we could see everything, and the band delivered. I'd seen the real Rolling Stones four times, and these guys performed the hits really well; they even did some rare tunes like "All Down the Line" and ended the show with an encore of "Satisfaction." It was all good, and I figured everyone was probably too beat to do the palm reading thing. I, for one, had no intention of bringing it up.

"Well? Are you chicken or what?" Chimed Mike after the encore and the house music returned to the speakers.

Continuing to be stunned by the thoroughness of his betrayal, I answered, "Not a problem. Let's go. Do you girls still want to do this?"

"Absolutely. I believe in this stuff, and horoscopes, too. It's all real," Jackie chimed in.

"OK, let's go; I don't know what anyone wants to bet, but I'm not afraid of anything, except winning too much money and having to claim some taxes."

And off we went, down the street to Madam Pearl's House of Magic.

***

OFF TO MADAME PEARL'S

Our group was a bit hammered, ears still ringing, and extremely curious when we rolled up to the "magic shop", as I kept calling it, much to the misery of the girls who were, for all intents and purposes, full-on believers. It was a little after ten o'clock, at which time most of the storefronts in Georgetown were closed and the streets nearly empty, except for a few restaurants up Wisconsin Avenue.

The Madame's storefront looked so cheesy from the outside, I immediately thought of the wizard in the Wizard of Oz hiding behind his green curtain. *Pay no attention to the man behind the curtain. . .* blah blah blah.

In the window, this place had a purple felt curtain complete with sparkly stuff all over it, a drawing of a giant hand with lightning bolts around it, something that looked like a decrepit black cat, maybe a crow flying, and some round thing that must have been a crystal ball. I did realize I was a bit tipsy and the streetlight was dim, so I might have been mistaken. But come-on! Did I mention cheesy? Well, it was. It looked like patrons could borrow the crystal ball to use as a disco ball at a house party!

"Are you guys sure you want to do this? I've had a great night. I say we hit up Whispers and get a drink, see if anyone's on tonight."

"Noooo! C'mon, you chicken, let's go." Sue was still hammering me on going in and that was enough for Mike and the others.

In they went, leaving me to ponder the benefits of the Irish exit until I relented and followed.

"Hellooooo, is anyone here? Are you guys open?" I chimed, faking eagerness.

This was a bunch of BS, and I could not believe I got roped in. Three steps in and I was already regretting I hadn't pulled the secret exit and jumped in a cab. This was starting to feel exactly like when I was a kid; my cousins were convinced Ouija boards were real and held spooky curses, and they were scared to death of them. Well, we *had* to have a séance, in which they did everything in their power to make the atmosphere *outside* of the game scary: dimming the lights, and checking the closets, lighting candles, making scary sounds and speaking in odd voices. Of course, nothing actually happened. Total nonsense.

Madame Pearl's place was all dark, and I was beginning to think it was closed and we were trespassing. Talk about something scary. . . We could be going to jail for a felony! My friends believed in things implicitly, on faith, sorta like kids, which was odd because I was the one into sports and cars, which they had been teasing me about all night. Anyway, the way I'm constituted was I have to see things to believe them—facts above superstition. Wizard stuff like Harry Potter was not on my bookshelves. I actually liked biographies and history books, not mumbo jumbo fantasy.

We all stopped in a room and came to stand around the center of it which had a table draped in a black cloth with some fold-up seats set up around it. A quick look about produced the following: everything was black, even the walls, which had a ton of shiny glittery stuff; it reminded me of when my sister decided to turn her room into an astrology tent with stars, moons, and planet stickers pasted all over the place. There was a round table with a crystal ball (yes, a crystal ball) right in the middle of it, all covered by a felt tablecloth. This room was eerily similar.

"Helloooo," I crooned with feigned interest, "are Vincent Price and the wax guys around? Paging Mr. Price. Mr. Price…"

"Billy, cut it out. Somebody's coming!" Susie said.

"Yeah, Billy, c'mon, be cool," the agreeable wingman on a mission unhelpfully added. I really had to hand it to Mike; he was working this agreeable thing to levels I didn't think were possible. Well, the girls were extremely good looking. And if I didn't think this stuff was so fake and need to teach these dummies a lesson, I might actually have had to become agreeable, too.

"Yes? Can I help you?" said a sweet looking, old lady, dressed like a gypsy. Or a pirate. Or a hippie who was lost. She had on a purple bandana, giant hoop ear-rings, several rings on her hand (the largest of which was a red ruby—probably fake), and a necklace with several circle clasps with pictures inside, probably of Linda Blair after things went south in the "Exorcist." The pictures I couldn't actually make out, because my vision was not the best, but I could guarantee that it was something dumb.

"Yes, hello, are you Madame Pearl?" said Maureen. "We are very interested in getting our palms read, maybe doing some tarot cards, or does the crystal ball do anything?"

"Only sees into the future, if that means anything to you my dear. Come closer. Let me see you. And, yes, I'm Madame Pearl. I've been working here for forty years, and before that, my mother worked for over fifty years in the old country, Bulgaria. We've been blessed in seeing things others don't for over eighty years."

"Excellent!" said Sue.

"Ok, how much do things cost?" I asked as sweetly as I could.

Even though it was clearly a scam, this lady looked like my grandma from Brooklyn and I didn't want to offend her, at least not overtly. I wondered if cookies were going to be involved in this if things went well.

"It costs twenty dollars for a palm reading, five dollars for the crystal ball, and if anyone's interested, I can do a séance for all of you for one hundred and fifty dollars."

I couldn't help but notice she was looking directly at me, almost as if she was trying to see if I was interested in the big dealio or just the palm reading, or maybe it was to scrutinize me. Perhaps I was not hiding my skepticism well.

"I believe we have a non-believer," Madame Pearl said as if to answer my thoughts.

"I am not sure what I believe," I stammered.

I was in a bit of a balancing act, trying to hedge my disbelief in a palatable way. I have to admit, the girls were easy on the eyes, but this stuff I simply did not want to give the time of day.

"Horoscopes, cards especially, all of it. Didn't Houdini the famous magician catch people all the time trying to scam people with this stuff? I need to see it to believe it."

If only I knew just how expensive my skepticism and need to be right was going to be, I might have just played along. But I can't help myself sometimes, and this affair was definitely evidence of that.

"Well, I believe, Madame Pearl. I'd like to get my palm read. I believe these are good ways to see the future." This from Mike. *He has no pride.* Enough said.

"And can we get ours read, too? How much was that séance thing?" This from Susie. *Lord help her clients when she starts practicing law someday.*

Madame Pearl was looking right at me as if she heard my thoughts on Susie. "Well, young man? Are you going to join your friends in this quest for knowledge, too?"

I was being challenged but wanted to get my money's worth.

"Since we're dealing with the supernatural, can we please see if we can get a spirit of somebody famous to pop in and join us? I want to ask Jim Morrison what exactly happened. Is there any kind of directory of spirits we can call? Can we ask him if he knows of any good tribute bands of the Doors coming to the Washington DC area soon?"

I tried not to let my sarcasm leach out, but perhaps I didn't do the best job. She clearly was not amused by my questions.

"Young man, this may seem like a game to you, but this is how I earn my living, and I think you should remember that. And didn't you learn to respect your elders? I do not have a personal set of spirits to call; this is not how it works. *I* read off of *you*, and we see what your aura brings us."

"Oh. Ok, I thought you could call spirits. My bad. I just asked because I heard much of this stuff is fake, and I thought if you called a ghost or two, it would prove it's real."

Madame Pearl gave me a smug look and the girls, followed by Mike, who was closely watching the girls, gave me a look that said *shut the ef up.*

"How's about I see how theirs all go, and I'll go last," I said, as an attempt to smooth things over.

I wondered if there was some way to expose any fakeness.

"Anyway, I'm getting it, too. Twenty bucks is not much, maybe I can get some hints on lottery numbers? Or tell if my company at work is going to merge with somebody? If so, this information is what I'm hoping to get."

So, one by one we all went:

When it was Susie's turn, Madame Pearl said, "You, my child—I see a very long life line, with much success, in some sort of industry that uses, I'm looking, it seems like some place with wood all over it, it's very nice….Maybe it's a…."

"A courtroom?" Susie chimed.

"Yes, I think it is! And you are speaking, in a very serious voice, looking like you are in charge of something, or some grave decision."

"I am amazed! That is exactly what I'm working for!" Susie was clearly buying the routine.

I sighed and thought to myself, *this can't be happening.*

Up next came the other girls, one by one, each getting some glowing descriptions of what's to come, and everything was positive and shining. I had to admit, I'd rather have this lady say good things rather than something gloomy, but I still didn't believe any of it.

Then came Mike. I had to really work to keep from laughing; I knew what he wanted his fortune to say, and I wondered if anyone else here had the same vibe I was getting.

I could make money too, if I told people what they *wanted* their future to be. At least this client. Madame Pearl would have to have some seriously broken radar going on; Mike kept checking out Jackie. I wonder if she saw that.

"I see someone who's very patient, probably you work with children. Or perhaps, are you a veterinarian?" Madame Pearl sweetly said. She liked Mike, he was an ally to her and apparently that's all it took.

"You're very perceptive; I have several nieces and nephews I help my sister with, and I love animals. Especially puppies," Mike eagerly responded.

This was playing well with the girls, obviously. I had to admit I was impressed. I knew he was as being as fake as I believed Madame Pearl's powers were.

I knew for a fact he did not like kids, and he wouldn't watch my dog once when I was in a jam and tried to pay him fifty bucks. Granted my dog is a boxer (named Rusty after Rusty Staub, a great NY Met, I might add), and a handful. But Mike did not know that, he just wouldn't watch him.

Ok, I will not torpedo him; in fact, I may help him write his acceptance speech when he wins an Oscar for this. If they hand them out at Madame Pearl's House of Scams. At least I kept my thoughts to myself. Although, if anyone had a sense of humor, I was missing out on wooing them.

"I knew he was a nice guy!" I had no idea who that came from, I was mesmerized by the performances and lost in the idea of Mike accepting the Pearl Award for best actor. And Madame Pearl herself being awarded a lifetime achievement award.

"Well, Mr. Non-Believer? Are you ready?"

"Absolutely; I am. I am very eager to see what is in my future and am very open to anything that can help me overcome my reluctance in believing this stuff. Except for the séance; I really don't want to see any ghosts tonight, especially for 150 dollars."

"Well ok, I will gladly read your palm, and since you are a bit of a skeptic, perhaps I can convince you? By hypnotizing you?"

"Uhhhhh, what? No way." This lady may not have been Houdini, but no way was anybody hypnotizing me; that stuff I actually believed might be true. God knows what I might say, or if she made me cluck and walk around like a chicken or turn into a dog. And who knows, what if I got stuck like that? No way.

"Well, then it seems you aren't such a skeptic after all; let me see your palm."

So, I turned over my hand and she started following the lines and mumbling to herself.

"Oooooh, these lines are very long and twisting; I feel you are conflicted; is there something bothering you? Perhaps are you nervous in the presence of these three beautiful girls?"

"No, that's not it; I might be nervous if I actually believed this stuff." Was I nervous? I thought not; I knew I wasn't the brightest bulb in the box, but I was funny. It works well when it works.

"Welllll, let's see; you see this line?" She pointed to a scar by my pinkie, which was from a long-ago bike crash. "It means you are inconsiderate and not thoughtful."

"Or a bad bike rider; that's a scar! I knew this was a scam. I will pay my cash, but there is no way this is real. That one proved it. And by the way, I actually do like dogs, otherwise the one at home who ate my eighty dollar shoes this morning would be in the pound. What else you got?"

Just then, Marissa from the Crazy Horse came in. "Hi Grandma! Is this one giving you a hard time? I know he thinks this is not real."

Thanks Marissa; I wondered if she realized I was the one who said we should give her twenty-five percent of the bill for a tip? Guess not. Also "Grandma?" Anyway, I had bigger fish to fry at that moment.

"He doesn't? Well, young man, if you think all of this is fake, how's about a challenge? Perhaps a dare?"

"No way; I'm out of here."

"Wait, Billy," chimed Maureen. "You talked big all night, said you'd bet everybody, and now you're afraid of Madame Pearl? I will bet you twenty bucks you can't complete the challenge she has for you."

"I don't even know what she's proposing."

"He's a chicken." This from Sue. "And he made fun of his really nice friend Mike. And Mike, are you seeing anyone?"

Good God, the hits keep coming.

"OK, hit me with it; just don't hypnotize me. I need to get home tonight, and I'd really like to do it walking on my two feet, not on all fours like my dog. I am not afraid of anything in this place. Hit me. What do you have? Some spell that's gonna make me fly around like a bat? What do you have?"

"Well," she sustained, as she reached onto a shelf to grab some gigantic book. That thing looked like a bible from the 1700s; one of those giant fat old things that should be in a vampire movie.

"Oooooooh noooooo," I sarcastically chirped. I could tell Madame Pearl was starting to get worked up.

"This is my spell book, passed down over the years from my great grandmother, to my mother, and now to me. One day, I will pass it on to my sweet granddaughter. Hopefully she will have the sense to stay away from petty non-believers. Let me look for something appropriate."

Then she flipped through the voluminous text (*probably a cookbook*) for about ten minutes as the girls and Mike chatted and Marissa shot me dirty looks from behind Madame Pearl. I kept quiet and was ready to get outta there. The night had been good, but this was turning into a loss and everyone was against me for, what amounted to, no good reason.

"No, that won't do," Madame Pearl shook her head and turned the page.

Marissa, leaning over and pointing said, "Well, he deserves this one."

And her Grandma the Witch actually sorta took my side, "But maybe one of these nice young ladies likes him, so I can't do that one."

"Nobody turns people into frogs anymore; that won't do, grandma."

I laughed out loud at that one, but Marissa looked up at me and wrinkled her nose, so I cut myself off. She looked cute as heck, and I didn't want to piss her off too much, but I knew I couldn't give in to this tripe.

"Is this going to take long? I mean, everyone knows this is fake and a scam," I said. I was starting to get tired, and this baloney was not getting us any closer to going home.

"*This* one will do; yes, it's quite appropriate for this young man. Well, are you ready?" Madame Pearl slyly asked.

"Please. I just saw some clown pretend he was Keith Richards, and I can play 'Brown Sugar' better on my own guitar. Hit me," I said.

And I wish now that I hadn't.

Pearl lit a candle, got a handful of some dusty stuff, threw it into the air above me, and said the following:

"For the next seven days, and the next seven nights, every horoscope for thee, will come into sight."

"That's it? Horoscopes? I thought you were going to turn me into a cat," I smartly said as I looked at my friends, all of whom looked worried and none of whom were laughing with me.

"Grandma, he's really not that bad, are you sure?" this from Marissa; maybe somebody did tell her about the tip. *Yes, it was me who said 25%.* I sent that thought over to Marissa and Madame Pearl in case they were eavesdropping. Anyway, I always tipped well, besides, she was kind of cute, too. Who knew, maybe if things didn't work out with these three girls, maybe Marissa and I could go out.

"Yes. This young man clearly thinks he's a shmizaburg."

"A what?"

"We called smart-alecky young men, shmizaburgs back in the old country. Well this one is going to learn some respect. I am tired. Marissa, you can take some cookies, the rest of you, it's twenty dollars each. I am closing up my shop."

We paid up, and promptly left; Mike and Jackie were off to the side chatting closely. I was impressed. That's why he was good at sales. Maureen and Sue had to do something early, and I was beat, so we decided to all head home.

"I wonder if that curse is gonna come true." Sue said

"No way, there's no way. She thought my scar was some kind of palm line."

We all walked the few blocks to the Metro and said our goodbyes. I took the Orange line home. Mike and Jackie grabbed an Uber cab and were going to get another drink. The other girls got on their respective lines. I had to admit, the evening was fun, if but a little wacky with the palm reading lady, though I was sure nothing was going to happen with my horoscopes. The girls (including Marissa) were spunky; and that's always been a plus with me, so, who knows, we may be going out again, is what I was thinking on the train ride back.

"Goodnight Billy! Don't be afraid to read your horoscopes!!" Sue called over her shoulder.

I had to laugh; these girls were definitely great to hang out with, and we decided by text to maybe hit another club next week. I was thinking about what the future would hold meeting those ladies again as I exited the train at Reston and found my car.

***

SATURDAY
This Dog Won't Hunt

Saturday morning my head was pounding me.

"I probably shouldn't have had that last margarita," I said to my dog, Rusty.

I used to party pretty hard, but not so much anymore. When I did have a wild night, I usually paid for it. Still, the night was fun, and when I checked my cell phone, I already had a text from Mike saying Jackie had already texted *him* that the girls had a great time and wanted to do something again soon.

Not this weekend, I thought as I forced myself to sit up in bed and thought about my coffee downstairs and feeding Rusty who'd been patient enough. *I'm beat.* I usually moved slow on Saturday mornings, and, that morning, I was moving margarita slow.

The best part about Saturday mornings? Not having to be anywhere–work, school, stores, obligations, nowhere. In today's world, everybody needs to do everything, be here and there, lunch, taking photos, and basically Facebook this and Twitter that, but not me. Saturdays (and Sundays) were for goofing off and relaxing. So, I rolled out of bed at some time between 8am and 10am—I didn't keep track of time on weekends—and headed downstairs to get a cup of coffee, maybe check out the sports scores, or get some news, and figure out my day.

My house was a three-level townhouse in Sterling, Virginia; nothing fancy or exotic, just a bread and butter outside-of-DC townhouse with some nice features and amenities which I shared with my dog Rusty (an eighty-pound boxer). If you know anything about boxers, it's that they're jumpy and enjoy licking faces, while also being great watchdogs, and just a bit crazy.

He definitely kept up the boxer reputation. He was full of maybe too much energy, but still a great dog who I'd adopted as a rescue. But not so great that morning. *Please no jumpiness* I thought before and while he kept licking my face (after jumping and barking several times). I pushed him off and then he jumped back striking the end table where my coffee sat poised above the carpet. Thank God I was able to grab it as I sat down. Despite the booze and late night, I still had some solid reflexes.

I tossed Rusty one of his chew toys a few times (an indestructible fish) and he took off to my basement to pummel it while I sat down and caught the news on tv. Nothing huge happened: there was a small house fire in Louduon County (my county). Thankfully no one hurt, a spot about some bus strike possibly in DC, and that was it. Good. Nothing heavy. I could catch up on sports without worrying about the world crumbling around me.

Since it was April, the baseball season had started and the Mets were off to a great 6-2 start, two games ahead of the Nats.

"As usual," I muttered to myself through the coffee mug as I took a steaming gulp.

If any of last night's peeps had been around, I would have let them have it for supporting the Nationals, Washington, D.C.'s unreliable baseball team. I made a mental note to chide the group of girls on the Nat's failures the next time we went out.

Neither team played last night, so I wasn't really caring about the scores as Rusty came back upstairs, ready for shenanigans and more jumping. Did I mention Saturday's were Rusty's day? Because, even if I didn't think so, he sure as heck acted like it.

As many responsible dog owners do, they get their pets trained; in fact, we signed up for this six-class course at PetPal to do just that— get trained. And it was not good; we lasted three classes because Rusty was nuts, and I was probably not the best student myself. I did not like being told what to do (definitely not on the weekend!), and apparently neither did my dog.

What I usually did was take him for long, high-energy walks during the week after work, and more intense park outings on nice weekends, which that post-margarita Saturday was turning out to be. We usually hit Algonquian Park for a run. Which, that day, I was lauding to myself as a great hangover cure; healthy and a good, productive start to the weekend. Or so I thought. . .

I just wanted to get the paper, give it a quick read, then off we'd go to the park. Just as I opened the door to get my paper, my eighty-pound friend blasted past me. It was like he was shot out of a cannon. He was free and running fast.

"Holy shit!" I said to myself, or maybe not as my next-door neighbor stood up from his bushes and said, "Hi Billy, is everything ok?"

"Uhh. No. Rusty just bolted out the door and I need to get him. He's by the mailboxes, please keep an eye on him while I get my shoes on."

"Ok!"

Alright, I thought. *No big deal.* Rusty had run out before and he always waited for me and the leash. I put my shoes on in a snap and thank God I was already dressed—a Saturday morning habit I inherited after many scoldings from my folks, I suppose. Normally if this happened, I'd grab his leash and some dog treats, which I typically kept by the door, but I hadn't rehung the leash! And the treat jar was empty. I didn't recall having neglected either. I always kept things in order. But there was no time for wondering about the hows and whys of my situation (did I eat the treats myself last night while hammered? Did Rusty eat his leash?); I needed to get him before he ventured too far.

One thing about boxers is they're actually pretty smart and if good ol' Rusty realized I was off my game, he'd run off fueled by his boundless energy and penchant for mischief.

Rusty saw me heading down the front steps and must have seen the look of weariness on my face, because he took off running fast as a racehorse across the street through my neighbors' yards, with me in hungover pursuit. I was not what you would call a really good runner. I was a wrestler in high school, and the only time I ever ran was to make weight for matches, or in baseball and softball, running bases (and we all know there are plenty of out of shape, slow guys in baseball). I'm quick enough in short bursts, but not built for endurance runs *or* catching fast-ass crazy dogs.

My plan (as I was trying to keep Rusty in eyesight) was to nonchalantly close the gap, and maybe corner him into a backyard with a fence. And this dog was just smart enough to realize it. Or was just devil enough to decide to torture me that morning, because he would bolt and get a huge distance between us, kind of slow down and wait, and when I'd get about fifteen feet from him, he'd look back at me, and take off anew.

This pattern took us through several streets and several other neighbors, and people were coming out of their houses, some with *really* helpful tips and observations.

"Hey, is that dog over there yours?" *No, I'm just running after it like a psycho for sport.*

"There he is, by those trash cans." *Glad you thought I looked blind.*

"Don't you know we have leash laws?" *Yeah, this was my protest march against the tyranny of community leaders.*

"Yes, thanks," was all I managed, out of breath and muscles spasming.

Apart from the outward politeness and the secret rage, what really was going through my head was that near my subdivision was a four-lane road called Algonquian Parkway, on which the speed limit was 45mph, and everybody pushed 60. The only good thing about that crazy morning was my dummy dog was running on a trail we often took to get to the park near my house where we usually went for long walks. The only bit of mercy he was having on me was he hadn't veered towards that busy road; he was just tearing through yards (flower beds be damned) leading to the park.

"Is that your dog in my flower bed? You know, it took me a long time to get it just right." That was the hot divorcee several houses down who I was waiting for my chance. Seemed like no such chance would come now. *Thanks, Rusty.*

"Yes, I'm sorry. He's loose and I'm trying to catch him," I shouted from across the street, trying to catch my breath before I made my move to snag the mutt. "Maybe try and grab him, if you can."

"Does he bite?"

"No, but he's jumpy and quick as they come."

Just then, a man came out the front door and all hope was really lost. Not for the dog, but for me and this woman. She asked him to snag the dog and he loped down the stairs and made too-direct a play for Rusty.

Well, the guy apparently was a Washington Redskins fan, because he tackled just like they do, in other words, not at all, and Rusty easily got away. At least he kept running toward the park and now we were just a half a block away and distancing ourselves from the parkway. And at least that street was one where he was at less risk of getting hit by a car.

I took a quick mental inventory of the park: It had woods, a boat launch, trails, and a golf course (outstanding hot dogs, too, which I'd enjoyed with this same dummy on happier walks; not this torture-run he was taking me on).

Anyway, his running pattern had not changed: slow down, wait till I'm close, make eye contact, and take off again.

"Heeeere Rusty! C'meere boy! If you stop right now, I promise steaks, hot dogs, your own roooom!"

I felt like I was negotiating with a teenager who had the upper hand.

"Remember we stopped those crappy lessons with the teacher who yelled at us both?" The irony of that fact wasn't lost on me, even if my dumb dog didn't get it.

Not even a woof, just the same look that said, "You must be kidding. We both know the deal; I'm having fun with this new game; you try to get close, I let you think I'm stopping, then I take off again!"

All throughout the park Rusty kept this up I didn't know at the time, but, to boxer dogs, this was a game. They liked you to chase them. They let you get close, then take off again.

As we ran through the park and onto the 4th hole of the course (and heard several *really good* suggestions, all of which I wish I could have answered if I wasn't so exhausted), and still the chase went on.

I glanced down at my watch, 10:45, and realized we'd been at this at least 40 minutes.

"Is he ever going to get tired?"

"Isn't there any way he might want to stop?"

"He can't possibly keep this up."

And I began to seriously question if I could even catch him; he was literally running like a racehorse. And then he was heading to a different hole and going to meet several more "patient friends" who were golfing.

"Hey buddy, I'm sorry, can you please grab him? He doesn't bite."

I'd regained some wind and called over to the party at the 7th hole.

Another Redskins fan, apparently, because another horrible "tackle."

The only good thing about my situation, was we were getting closer to the clubhouse, which meant farther from the road, so I had that going for me. *Maybe he remembers the hot dogs*, I was hoping. Maybe they had tranquillizer guns behind the counter. Maybe I'd never get the newspaper again without having him restrained like Hannibal Lector.

All I knew was I was making every deal I could think of with God while keeping my dummy in sight. No more smoking (I quit anyway, years before, but promised again to keep quit), no more cursing, especially the big ones (and had to retract a few of the ones I let go on the 4th hole), and a promise in general to just be better. I even offered to stop going to casinos from time to time (I was prepared to move this offer up the ladder of importance if I didn't catch the mutt soon).

Excellent, we were getting closer to the clubhouse, and he was doing a trot/run thing now, so I figured he was actually tiring. There seemed to be a lot more cars than normal parked in the visitor lot, and flowers arranged in an arch leading up the path. I couldn't see it entirely, and honestly was still half-jogging, so everything was bouncing in my eyesight, anyway.

I wondered what the flowers and myriad parked cars could be about until the mystery ended when I got closer. A wedding. *Oh, thank God!* I thought it was just going to be golfers pissed at me but now it was a wedding party and I knew, of course, weddings loved random stray dogs running amok during the ceremony…. *Really not good!* I was repeating to myself under my breath. A wedding meant brides/maids/moms/grandmothers. *OK, ok, maybe it will be fine?* Somebody there had to like dogs. Maybe the groom was a trainer. Maybe even the lady at PetPals where we quit the damn class was the bride!

Rusty, true to my thinking, must have remembered the hot dogs, because he ran around the neatly placed white folding chairs, making sure not to knock over any or jump his dirty paws on the seats, on his way to where the hot dog vendor usually was. I was getting closer now, approximately fifteen yards behind him. There were some people seated, but the wedding party was not up front yet, so it hadn't started (maybe my deals with God carried some weight). Rusty sniffed at an older couple who patted him nicely then headed to the front of the clubhouse, and I was praying that he gets inside somehow, where I could get him enclosed and caught. And true to my luck, he ducked inside as a door opened.

Perfect! I'd be able to catch him now, and I bolted to the door. At that point, I was relieved and sure I'd find him and corner him.

As soon as I got inside, however, I heard some plates break, and a loud "STOP THAT DOG!" followed by an even louder "OOOHHH NOOOOO!"

My mind raced for the half second it took to get into the kitchen, covering several dozen scenarios as if plotlines in a movie.

Rusty was lying on the floor (unhurt), but surrounded by icing, yellow cake, and two figurines that, judging by their wedding attire, used to sit neatly on top of the cake-now-mess before it ended up on the floor.

"Oh my God," was all I could get out, echoing the shouts I'd heard before arriving on the scene.

Then, as a big caterer closed in on Rusty, and looked like he was going to jump him, I said, "If you hurt my dog, you're going to think Mike Tyson's been invited to this wedding; just let me get him." And I pounced. He was exhausted by then, anyway, and cornered.

As I wrestled Rusty to the ground with a dog-squeal and a few licks to my face, I noticed a large, seething shadow cross over us. I was naively happy that I'd caught the stupid mutt and that barely anything had happened. A cake? Big deal. But, obviously I hadn't thought clearly. I had a very big and new problem as the father of the bride had arrived in time to see the mess, the dog, and myself in the middle of it. I thought to myself, *great, it doesn't get any better than this, unless the bride shows up and starts crying.*

"Whaaaaat? That's the cake?" the father growled. "Whose dog is that?"

"Umm, that would be me." I was praying that the real Mike Tyson was coming to this wedding and was a dog lover.

Father looked like he was going to explode, maybe even reach for the butcher's knife and come at me or Rusty. I had to say something to alleviate the situation.

"Sir, I am terribly sorry. I don't know what to say, but please give me a chance to fix this, before you get the police, knock me, or my dog out. Believe it or not, I think I can."

"You have two minutes. Speak. And make it good, or the law is coming."

The only *potential* plan I could think of was my Aunt Nancy. She'd worked as a caterer for some time. If I could get a hold of her, she might connect me to a baker. Hail Mary, here we go.

"Sir, my aunt's a caterer, she knows several bakers, and what if I can get another cake here? The wedding hasn't happened yet, we have some time before the reception, it seems. Please let me try. I'll even give the bride and groom a wedding gift. If this works, we'll all have a good story for years. That is if I don't have heart failure first."

"I reserve the right to have you arrested if we don't have a solution in ten minutes; my daughter has been the definition of the Bride-Godzilla thing and she and her mother both are driving me to drinking. They are each going to go nuts when they see this, if I even let them know. You have ten minutes, son, and it better be the best ten minutes of yours and that damn dog's lives. Make the call."

Off I went on another race; this one was less a marathon and more of a sprint to the phone in the kitchen. Rusty had been secured behind the kitchen with rope and several bowls of water, and a couple of hot dogs. (I hoped he wasn't considering this a reward; we were still not out of this mess).

After explaining the story to my Aunt, she told me to tell the gentleman she could have a cake there in an hour. I was stunned. She was going to a catering expo in Centerville (close to us) with three of her bakers later today and were taking two cakes. Each were those big, three-layer things with white icing, and she swore to me they looked nice. She took two quick pics on her cell phone and sent them to the lead caterer, who showed them to the father, and he approved. I immediately thanked everyone and planned on buying lottery tickets on the way home because I'd never been that lucky in my life. That is, assuming, of course, I didn't have a nervous breakdown before the end of the day.

Well, true to her word, my Aunt Nancy brought the cake up there, (the wedding still hadn't started), and both parents of the bride were ok with the new cake. We just cleaned off the figurines and replaced them on top, good as new. I told my aunt I'd pay for the cake ($250!), and also told the parents my wedding gift was still coming, and, at that point, they said no worries, that it wouldn't be needed.

I always had a special place in my heart for my aunt, and now I remembered why. She always cared for me, in a way someone does that is always in your corner. She was and will always be my favorite person from my parents' generation.

So, with that, I thanked everyone, took Rusty on his new "rope leash," and walked home, avoiding the park altogether and keeping my crazy dog close to my side the whole way.

When we arrived home, my neighbor was glad to see I caught Rusty, though he heard from his wife half the block had already been on the phone to complain about wild dogs wrecking gardens. I asked him to keep my identity hidden from the authorities and, at long last, picked up my paper and headed in to, finally, begin (again) my Saturday. The way it was supposed to be: a cup of coffee and the paper. So, it was 2:15 now, Rusty was in the house, and all was secured. I sat in my reading chair with some reheated coffee and opened the paper prepared to luxuriate in what was left of my afternoon.

After reading the sports section and a few items in the metro section, I got this notion to check the horoscopes. In all the excitement I totally forgot about it.

I had to jog my memory of the zodiac and signs and all that mumbo jumbo. My birthday was August 4th, same as Roger Clemens, John Riggins, and even President Barack Obama. If only I had a Met on my day, too, it would be even better. Anyway, it turned out I was a Leo.

LEO
"Today's race will be long and it will be far,
but don't worry you'll win, because YOU are a star!
Life is a journey and sometimes fun, don't rest easy,
though, your challenge has hardly begun!
...Remember, you can't have your cake and eat it too."

I thrust the paper down, picked it up and read it again. A long race? Cake? Far? A challenge?

I had to stop myself from getting involved. There was no way that lady could have planned any of what just transpired; like everyone says, horoscopes are so generic they can be applied to anything! The only thing miraculous about the last 24 hours was the girls thought Mike was one of those "sensitive" guys who likes puppies and small children. Christ. What a bunch of baloney. The only dog Mike liked was himself; he was a hound. But he was still my best friend. Mostly a harmless hound. Maybe I was overthinking things, but the horoscope had me on edge. What if all this was real?

Whatever. There was no way that lady's spell was real. It had to be a coincidence. It had to be. No other rational explanation.

Anyway, after that whole morning I didn't want to get worked up. I wasn't sure what I believed and decided to think about it later. Right then, I was pretty beat after running all over the place, and decided on taking a well-deserved nap, and thinking more on the genie or whatever she was, witch or sorceress, after a good rest.

Little did I know then that no nap would have covered the rest I was going to need for the next week.

***

SUNDAY
The Helpful Handyman

Looking back now, I realized I was much more tired than usual. I guess chasing a dog on a marathon run, all the time wondering if magic was possible will do that to you.

Consequently, my nap was much longer than I thought. I woke up at 5PM and decided that it really was just my mind playing tricks on me—*no way are magic spells real*, and no way were Saturday's shenanigans related to anything other than a dummy (that would be me), letting another dummy (Rusty the dog with endless energy) escape. Did I need a treadmill? I didn't think so. Just every once in a while, let the dog loose and I should be ready for the Boston Marathon in no time.

Anyway, I had bigger fish to fry. My parents, who were in their 60s (Mom) and 70s (Dad), needed a hand with some things around their house. Or, more realistically, my Mom wanted me to lift heavy stuff for my Dad, since he wouldn't listen to her, and just does stuff he probably shouldn't—like climb up the world's most dangerous ladder to get onto his roof, to clean out the gutters. I didn't like using it, and I doubted Spiderman, if he was real, would either. But in all fairness to him, my Dad always managed to do various projects without hiring the professionals and jobs somehow ended up completed. They may not always have looked the best, or got done in a timely fashion, but they got done. I respected him for always finishing the job.

So, Sunday morning I bounced up at 7 AM, had a cup of coffee, and, just to cover all my bases, got my paper with the dog locked away,

32

and turned straight to my horoscope just to be on the safe side.

LEO

*"Making a splash is the best thing you do,
So please remember, it's ok to be you.
And don't be alarmed as you get set,
the worst that can happen is you might just get wet!"*

What could come from a horoscope like that? I thought that was one of the most vague and ridiculous sounding ones ever. Typical. I was totally in the clear. I put down the paper thinking, *OK, I'll be only me.* I didn't know who else I could be and wondered what kind of writer they got for these things.

Now, I had to confess that on special occasions, I did like to be someone else. Who didn't? The biggest chance to be someone else was Halloween, my favorite holiday of all, and even though I was way too old for trick or treating, I still did the costume thing at parties or bars each year. In fact, one year I came in 2nd place in a bar contest as Captain America. I lost to two very deserving young ladies who went as the best dressed police officers I had ever seen. What a great holiday.

But I was getting caught up in my imagination and didn't want to stay in that space too long. That's the space in which my friends existed, apparently, with their silly beliefs in magic and sorcery and curses and such. I had a bunch of things I needed to do, the first of which was drive to Vienna from Sterling (both in Northern Virginia), and that was about 25 minutes. I told my mom I'd be there at 9 to give them a few hours. I needed to be home by 4PM, however.

For this trip, I planned on rolling out the rocket, my toy, a 1973 Ford Mustang fastback I was restoring. This car was absolutely non-essential. It was old, got bad gas mileage, had bad paint, but got one thing that excused all that: a 429 Super Cobra Jet engine under the hood, with a 4-barrel carb, and an oversized cam. And over 400 horses of power. Another plus was my dad loved this car, and we always had great fun talking cars.

I didn't know much about the cam, but I did know a 4-barrel is a carburetor that pours (yes, pours) gas into the "Super Cobra Jet." And the horsepower? Fantastico. I wish I could have raced 400 real horses at once, or maybe have a tug of war to see if any of that was true. The paint? A horrible black that was so weathered it looked like it was flat, which made it look rough. Add in the dents, and this thing looked like Mad Max's car. In other words: awesome.

But mostly, this car was fun, and being a car guy, I loved it and the process of restoring it. Rusty was my dummy best friend, and this car was my baby. I had plans to fix it up in phases, and after that little wedding cake debacle, I now had to put off the paint job for a bit longer. I jumped in and eased it from the garage into the driveway where I parked it and let the engine hum fill the morning. *It runs great*, was all I could think listening to it purr. I loved the car and my Dad loved it too, so I had to bring it over. Rusty, I decided, had to come with me, and believe it or not, my Mom actually liked the 80-pound beast of a dog!

"He still thinks he's a lap pup!" she loved to say when he climbed on to the couch to get in her lap.

"No, he doesn't have to get down!" that was her reaction when I tried to rescue her from suffocation. Rusty looked forward to going to my parents just to feel like a pup again, I believed that to be true.

So, the trip was going to be a bit nuts, because, well, we had the dog galumphing around my mom's pristine house, and then my dad with his atypical approach to fixing things. And, being from a generation that cared more about sports, cars, and partying (let's not forget my friends and their belief in magic), I did not know how to be handy around the house. I was telling one of the ladies at work, nobody would mistake any of my projects with ones by the guys on "This Old House." Our tools were typically the hammer (can get you out of most trouble), duct tape (vital), putty, and paint. When I was younger, my biggest job was "hold the light"; as I've gotten older, I graduated to "hold the ladder," "can you see where that thing went," and the most important, "don't tell your mother": all of which I was more than capable of handling.

I personally got a bit of a bad home repair rap from my brothers; some of my best repair work had involved "unique, custom solutions". Like, for example, a pesky leak from the kitchen sink to the basement. For some reason, that pipe in the basement would leak horribly every once in a while, and one weekend (when I was home for the summer from college), my parents were away, leaving my brother and me at home.

That was the weekend I became a fan of epoxy. Epoxy looks like

Play-Doh (grey Play-Doh), and when it dries, it is like concrete. What is it made of? Magic (whoops, you caught me! I did believe in some magic, apparently). A small mountain of that stuff caked around that fat pipe in the basement made the leak history. Did it look pretty? Hell no. But was it visible? Another big fat no. It was in the corner of a basement with a bunch of other pipes, so I was satisfied with my handy work. It never leaked again is how I finish off any argument suggesting my craftsmanship was shoddy.

"That's some good work, son; that thing hasn't leaked in over a year." Even the old magician himself admired my resourcefulness.

I liked to think the epoxy-pipe story is why I continued to get these calls; it's "the epoxy effect." Either that, or I didn't think fast enough to tell my parents no and let them call my brothers.

So, I pulled into their driveway at about 9ish, and headed inside with the four-legged "angel." I found my parents in the kitchen having coffee with a list in front of them. It was never good when they had a list. That meant some thought has been put into whatever needed getting done. Thought meant a lot of work, let me tell you.

We said our greetings and my mom immediately took Rusty for a treat.

My dad was telling me about their social life when I picked up The List:

- Clean the gutters (this meant a battle with the "Death Ladder" to the roof)
- Bring up some boxes of junk to take to a landfill (cake, using a wheel barrel, could hammer out quickly)
- Fixing the side of the house storm door hinge (could be a pain, who knew)

All good. *This stuff should take three hours max, and I should be home by 4 PM easily.* I needed to do some stuff around my own house (some laundry, and get some groceries), and get ready to watch Sunday Night baseball. I had my priorities. Especially since I had some money riding on the game and, perhaps most importantly, bragging rights.

The first thing up was the gutter cleaning; my dad insisted on getting up there himself, using a tiny scoop for getting the leaves out, then nailing the gutter to the house to prevent it coming away from the side.

My parents' house was a two-story rambler, with the basement being underground, so we really didn't need to go that high; probably 10 or 11 feet. I once nearly fell off it when we put on a new roof, and probably would've been ok since they had a ton of bushes around the front. The backyard, however, was a bigger drop since their backyard was sloped. A fall from over there would not be good; regardless, the hardest part of this job was the climb up.

The ladder itself was serviceable with only one of the hinges broken. There were two hinges on it, and while one side was fine, the other side was gone, and in its place was rope. Yes, rope, to tie it together? I asked my dad about the functionality and he pointed with his thumb and grumbled, "No questions. Only holding."

Death Climb, here we go. I wondered if mom had seen this, would we still be climbing our version of the Matterhorn?

"Hold the ladder steady while I climb up, then you follow."

My dad was on his mission and wouldn't be deterred for his safety, much less mine.

"Sure thing…" *But who's holding it for me while I climb up?*

Every time we used it, I promised myself I'm buying him a ladder for X-mas, his birthday, or even my birthday, since it would be a gift really for me, but inevitably I forgot until the next time I had to climb it.

But things went smoothly. I had to admit, for a 76-year-old person, he still could climb. The trick to this maneuver was the transfer to the roof. There was a small pipe sticking out of the roof (to this day I have no idea what comes out of it or goes into it) which he grabbed and used to pull himself up. Spiderman's grandfather? I don't know, but he got up there. So, *I should be able to also...* The Flying Wallendas would have been proud of him.

"Son, when you're on the top of the ladder, grab this pipe. *Do not* tell your mother about this. Just get up that way."

Being nimble and keeping a good eye on the bushes in case things, or I, went south, I made it up.

This was by far the hardest part task number one—cleaning the gutter and nailing anything that's loose was literally 20 minutes. And it went perfectly, and soon we were maneuvering down. The first person down (that was, of course, me), had the more challenging descent.

"Hold the pipe till you feel your feet on the ladder, then *slowly* walk down a step or two, then let go of the pipe. When you get down, hold the ladder for me."

It was clear to me I was being used since he had been perfectly capable of handling all on his own and I wondered how this easy job became a "2-man mission." I decided I didn't want to get into it with him, and further decided, sealed with an unbreakable personal oath, to get him a ladder. Soon.

So, he climbed down, no issues, and we moved on to the rest of the list.

"Look at us, son. It's only 11 AM and we're rolling."

"Dad, why don't I get those boxes out to the curb, and you get your tools for that hinge repair."

"Good idea, I'll do that."

The boxes were cake; eight boxes for Vienna's Good Will and using the wheel barrel (no missing parts for once), I was done in fifteen minutes. Onto the next task, which was not too bad, either; the bottom part of it was loose, and this also was a two-person job: one guy to hold the door straight, (me), while the other tightened the loose hinge. The job was a cinch and I was thinking about a quick lunch, and then Rusty and I would be firing up the Mustang and bolting home.

We ate a quick few sandwiches, and I was ready to leave when my mom asked my Dad, "Joe, did you guys tighten that joint on the pool? The deck felt a little wobbly."

"Oh, I forgot. Billy, this will only take a few minutes, can you help me before you leave? I need to tighten the bracket holding the deck to the side of the pool."

Their pool was an old, above-the-ground model that my parents filled each year and never used. I suppose it was for us kids and the grandkids on occasion. Maybe they just like having the chore—really, chores and responsibilities bound them more than their vows. Anyway, the construction was pretty ingenious—a large, four-foot-high circle that one person could assemble and that stayed together via gravity and some brackets. Once the supports were standing, the liner was looped onto the top, and a hose filled it in two days.

The entrance deck piece attached to the side of the pool and provided a staircase to the flat top where a ladder dipped into the water. I'd done this job a few years ago and it was easy, ten minutes at the most, but a pain in the butt for one person to handle on their own. Mostly because there's a risk of falling in or wrecking the bracket. It was one thousand percent easier if someone held it while the other

37

person tightened it to the side. There were three braces under the deck that held it, and all we needed to do was tighten the bolts on the bottom, securing it to the pool wall, and it would then be rock solid.

"C'mon, son, let me get my pliers and a screwdriver. This'll take a second."

"Sounds good, dad. I'll be underneath prepping the site."

So, my dad went inside to his workbench and grabbed the tools and returned while I fiddled with the braces and noticed that they were, in fact, oddly loose.

"Hey, dad, anything happen to loosen the bolts?"

"Couldn't tell you. We haven't used it since last summer when your brother was here with the kids."

It seemed odd. The screws were made to stay in unless acted upon with a tool and a lot of force. I started to ask him some more questions, but he gave me the old thumb-point again and barked out his orders.

"What I need you to do is get to the braces at the bottom and tighten the three bolts with the pliers and we'll be done. I'll hold it steady and level on the top. Just don't overdo it."

Excellent. Tighten three bolts and I'm out. I could probably have done the job by myself, but he wanted to be a perfectionist about it. I could hear him already, "Janey, look at all this stuff I did, I even showed Billy how to fix things at his house."

Yes, that's right, 76 years old and still bragging about fixing stuff; well, I'd let him, no worries there. I was in the business of keeping those two happy and placated else one of 'em might be living in my basement.

So, starting from right to left, dad climbed the steps next to the deck, and held the bracing level and study to the side of the pool, and I tightened the first bolt easily. Literally three turns, and it was tight. Maybe ten seconds?

"This is going easy, keep holding it, I'm gonna do the second one."

Perfecto, just as easy as the first bolt; no wonder one person could put this ugly pool up by themselves. *I may get one of these when I get a house with a bigger yard.* I was thinking to myself and imagined hosting Mike and our lady friends for a pool party, with Rusty behaving like a saint and, you know what, Mike leaving early and the ladies sticking behind to spend time with me talking sports, cars, and rock bands!

I was brought out of my fantasy when my dad shouted, "Hey, get this third bolt done so I can let go. My hands need a break and it's almost time for our afternoon show."

"Dad, keep holding it and hold your horses. I'll do the last one, but it looks a little rusted or something." Something looked off about the bolt, but then I removed some crud from the fitting and got the screwdriver in their to give it a turn.

For this one, my dad got on the deck, in the middle of it, and held it tighter to make it perfectly flush. The only problem was that made the bolt jut out slightly and the angle a little more difficult to use leverage.

OK, this is one must've been the one that caused the entire thing to be loose, I was grumbling, because it needed more than three turns. Zero issue, though, just kept turning it, four times, hmm, but it started to catch and felt like the final turn and we'd be golden.

It was finally snug, and I had to admit, as easy as they said. I was looking forward to a public victory with my mom, "That deck is muuuuch tighter! Thank you."

"Son, tighten the ends good, they'll hold the whole thing steady."

"No prob." Bob Villa had nothing on me; I fixed stuff on the roof, some leaves and boxes and shit, now this thing…

So, I used the pliers on two of the minor bolts to the sides of the main ones and gave them a good crank. *One, two, three, and I'm outta here.*

Then I heard a small twinge on the bolt, figured it just needed another turn.

What I thought was the bolt that twinged, was really the thing I was tightening it into. A bracket. A rusty bracket that had a sharp edge and just cut a pinhole at the bottom edge of the liner.

What happened in the next millisecond I can only speculate; all I knew is I heard a loud "SWWOOOOOOOSHHHH" and was immediately hit by what I can only describe as a tsunami. How much water? I had no idea. How cold? Alaska cold. Hard, fast, and the next thing I knew I was 40 or 50 feet back towards the end of my parents' yard, in a heap, tangled in the low bushes. Water all around me, and I was soaking wet and tasted dirt in my mouth.

"Billy! Are you ok?"

Dad was holding onto what was left of the deck, looking like a shipwrecked sailor; somehow, *he* didn't get soaked or injured or move at all, but he was hanging on to the deck for his dear life. Rusty was barking like crazy inside. And my mom, I could see, had swiped open the curtains in the kitchen.

"I'm ok, just banged up. I don't think we should work on the pool anymore. In fact, the pool doesn't look too good."

I got up, and he climbed down to survey the damage.

The pool, one of my favorite things ever, where we had multiple water battles, volleyball games, even floating Wiffleball games, looked like King Kong stepped on it. Or at least one side of it; it was collapsed, crunched, and empty. And the water? Gone. Except for a few puddles in what was left of the pool.

How much water? The pool was 24-foot diameter, 52 inches deep, and held between 13,000 or 14,000 gallons of water, depending how it was filled. All I can say is it all shot out of the side like a cannon and knocked me on my ass and tossed me across the yard; it was like getting wrecked by giant wave at the beach, a cold ocean wave.

If there was any silver lining, it was that no one was hurt but for a few bruises and scrapes, and at least the backyard looked immaculate. I guess that's what 13,000+ gallons of fast-moving water would do for you. Every single stick, leaf, clump of dirt—all of it was spotless. Where did all the water go? Down the slope to a creek that ran along the edge of their property.

I had to look, so I ran down to the creek and yes, it was about three feet deeper than normal. I wondered if their neighbors would report the incident to the EPA; well, I wasn't gonna let this become a superfund site, that was for sure. Besides, it seemed to be moving downstream and my parents hardly used any chlorine.

"Honey, did you get splashed?" My mom was calling from the back door, and of course it was the understatement of the century. I was about to yell at her given my obvious state of nearly-been-drowned when it hit me: *Making a splash is the best thing you do…* My damn horoscope! This was two days, two horoscopes, and two disasters. I didn't know how (I think I knew the "why"), but this was getting nuts. How could this be possible? Did the old witch hunt down my parents and loosen the brackets or rust them out with some chemical hocus pocus? No. That would be impossible, right?

I was watching the water rush away down the creek and was beginning to worry for my future safety. I could not have this happen because I had too much stuff going on at work. I had to prepare for an "All Hands" call, some highly visible projects, and a trip to New York City later in the week.

Is this really happening? I needed to figure a way out, or just pray whatever happens wasn't too bad going forward. Dammit. On the one hand, there was no way some fake wizard could pull any of this off. And, I didn't believe in magic and karma and horoscopes! But, how else could I explain what happened? I had no one to talk to. Nobody was going to help me, much less believe me. Did I even want to tell anyone? They'd think I was nuts; in fact, I was starting to wonder if I was nuts. *Maybe I should call Mike and see what he thinks…*

"Billy, c'mon, the creek's not going anywhere, get over here. We need to figure out what we're telling your mother. This one's worse than when the tree fort fell down and hit the house. Get over here."

I trotted over and helped him down from the now, free-standing pool deck just as we heard:

"What happened out there?"

"Uhhhhh, we had a little issue, we may be needing a new one," My dad ventured, and, lower to me, "don't tell her you were swept all over the place, I'll never hear the end of it. You fell in fixing that floating chlorine tube. By the way, where is that thing?"

"It's in that tree over there."

"Quick, get it; and your Met hat's up there, too. Hurry up."

So, after a quick survey, my mother uttered,

"Are you sure you two didn't break something?"

She always found out about the duct tape and epoxy and half-assed repairs and figured we'd tried something dumb. If anything, my mom was the brains of the operation, and knew we were suspect repairmen. Or, disrepair men.

Then the cagey veteran took over:

"Absolutely not, I don't know how that thing broke. Maybe we should call a lawyer or somebody. That pool could've flooded the house if it went the wrong way. Thank God I steered the water toward the creek."

I decided I had enough excitement for one day and wanted to get going. My work (or non-work) there was done. It was time for me to make my escape before we tried to fix something electric.

"I need to get going, Dad. I'll come back next weekend and we can haul it to the landfill, maybe get a new one."

I gave them a quick hug, rounded Rusty up ("wait outside you'll get water all over the house"), and we headed home.

At least with the windows down, I would be a bit drier when I got home and sloshed in, wondering what tomorrow's horoscope would say. I was really looking forward to it since I had to go to work! Wedding cakes and swimming pools were nothing compared to things that might affect my livelihood.

All I could do was think, if this thing was real, maybe I'd get a good one like "go buy a bunch of lottery tickets" or "your boss loves your work" or "buy that car, you can easily sell it after you fix it up." Being an optimist, there had to be a good one coming.

Just as I pulled up, I decided to give my wingman a call and see if he thought I was going nuts, or just a victim of bad luck.

"Mike, are you there?"

He was one of those guys who still had a house line with an answering machine attached. He usually screened his calls that way and rarely answered his cell at home unless it was a text from a chick. Between multiple girls, and an unfortunate bet that went south, he needed to know who was calling him before he answered.

"Listen up dummy. It's me, Billy, and I need to talk to you. Some wacky stuff's been going on, involving that psychic."

Still no pickup.

"OK, what if I told you that hot waitress called and was asking if I had your phone number?"

Immediately I heard a voice—amazing what guys (myself included) would do when a girl was involved, or some intel on one we were interested in.

"Hey Billy, I'm sorry, I was asleep on the couch and juggled the phone trying to pick it up. So that waitress called you? How? Did you get her number that night? If so, touché, and well done. Now give it to me."

"I don't have it, but let's go back there for lunch later this week. I have some work in DC I need to do, and will have some time, but something weird has been happening the last two days, and it would be great if we could grab a beer."

"Alright pick me up in twenty minutes, let's go to Wilson's and get steaks. And if this is some sappy needy crap, you will be buying. And I'm telling you in advance, I am not watching that beast of a dog. You know I don't like dogs or kids either. So forget it if that's the deal."

"It's not dogs, kids, or anything else, dumbass. And no, I don't have any 'locks' to bet on either. I'll be there in twenty minutes."

I took Rusty inside my place, got him fed, and secured in the basement (he had, on occasion, gone wild when I was out). Let's just say it was best for all parties if he didn't roam the house. And no, I didn't use "the crate" thing like smart dog people; that thing looked too much like a cage, and while that dummy may have torn a picture or two off my walls (Joe DiMaggio and Johnny Unitas come to mind), he will never be caged in my house. He is not a parakeet.

Twenty minutes later, I pulled up in front of Mike's place.

"So, what's going on? And when are we eating in DC?"

"I have a big job at the Norwegian embassy coming up and need to work in DC on Tuesday. Let's grab lunch or dinner then, and we can go by her restaurant. And yes, I'll be a supportive wingman, despite you taking credit for the giant tip I suggested we leave her."

"Cool. Now what's so important?"

Just then, we pulled up in front of Wilson's, one of my favorite restaurants. Not only is there a ton of hot-looking girls, but the food is actually good. Wilson's is one of those new high-end steak places that have super thick steaks and the best complimentary bread, which they give you when you first arrive.

Typically, they had this little basket deal with some sliced bread, but what was money were these things called Willie rolls, which may as well have been donuts. Or, the middle of the donut; those things were round ball like donut holes and were unreal. And usually everybody pounded them down and left the bread.

Our waitress walked up, and yes, like all other girls in Wilson's (which is a highly valued happy hour spot), she was smoking hot. Both Mike and I look at each other in acknowledgement (and I might have been having some crazy supernatural crisis going on, but I was not blind). Life might have been getting nuts, but it still goes on; hot waitresses were never un-noticed. Spunky ones (like Marissa) got the highest marks.

"Can we please get a basket of just the Willie rolls, none of the other bread, and for me, a Budweiser?"

Mike ordered a pale ale on tap that's from a local microbrewery.

"What a great choice, I like that myself. I'll be right back with that and (she looked disapprovingly) your Budweiser."

It may as well have been dish water. Oh well, I didn't care. I was a Bud man.

After we get our drinks, I decided just to tell Mike, and not sugar coat anything.

"Mike, this horoscope thing may be coming true. The last two days, some really crazy stuff's happened, and it actually sounds like it's tied to my horoscopes."

"Whaaaaat? You actually believe that crap? I only said it because I was agreeing with everything they said, you know, like 'Operation Agree on All' like we did that other time. Which by the way, worked extremely well; I dated that girl for six months, and thought she was the one. What happened to you and that other girl?"

"Can we please focus on this? I have some crazy Exorcist shit going on and need to know if you think I'm going nuts. In the last forty-eight hours, I've had a wedding nearly ruined, almost had a heart attack chasing that idiot dog, some old man nearly knocked me out, and my parents' pool went tsunami on me. The only thing that didn't happen is my car explode, I lose my job, or get on the news. But what the heck? It's only Sunday; the week hasn't even started."

"Dude, you can't be serious; you don't actually think these things are coming true? Do you? Are you going to be the crazy friend we all talk about in ten years?"

"I don't know; I don't think I'm crazy, but some weird stuff's happened the last two days. Let me read you these things and you be the judge."

I pulled out of my pocket the two crumpled up parts of the newspaper with my horoscopes and read Saturday's horoscope to him:

"Today's race will be long and it will be far,
but don't worry you'll win, because YOU are a star!
Life is a journey and it can be fun, don't be scared of it
all, your challenge has begun!
You can have your cake and eat it too. "

I told Mike the entire day: how I woke up, Rusty escaped, ran all over the place, destroyed a wedding cake, all culminating with nearly getting killed by the bride's father. (And a mental note to myself; *I will get my Aunt Nancy the best Xmas card ever, and she will never lift anything heavy again if I have anything do to with it*).

"I told you not to get that stupid dog; however, chicks for some reason like dudes with dogs. I was going to ask you if I could borrow him to go to a dog park sometime. And wait a minute, don't you have Marissa's phone number for me?"

"Can we please stay on topic? Spells, chaos, and this horoscope thing? My mental state? And no, I don't have her number."

"Oh, I'm sorry man; please continue crying for me."

I gave him a look that meant I was serious and continued.

"*Then* the next day, this morning, I went to my parents' house to help with some chores. Listen to this horoscope from Sunday:"

> *"Making a splash is the best thing you do,*
> *So please remember, it's ok to be you.*
> *And if you're alarmed as you get set,*
> *the worst that can happen is you might just get wet!"*

I went through the day's events, and described fixing a bunch of junk, all ending with the pool busting and water going all over the place and getting hit with essentially a tidal wave.

"Dude, you can't be serious; I've seen you and your dad in action fixing stuff. Remember the tree fort that hit your parents' house? Didn't you and your dad build that death trap? Thank God it just hit your house; I thought it was going to hit my bike, after it nearly hit me coming out of the tree. My mom nearly wouldn't let me go over to your house after that. I had to lie and tell her you were the goofiest kid in school and had no friends, which she easily believed. I'm surprised your mother still lets you guys actually try to fix things."

"Well, she had no problem with it today, but I have to admit, some of these missions have been debacles, but that pool busted out like Niagara Falls; all I did was tighten a couple of screws and, the next thing I knew, I was soaked and airborne. It's a good thing I'm nimble and can hold my breath; I ended up in the bushes at like fifty miles an hour; soaking wet, too."

"Ok, what is more likely? You and your dad busting stuff trying to fix it, OR some voodoo spell thing, that some hack zapped on you? And the wedding cake deal? I've seen that beast of a dog of yours in action; he doesn't need spells to be nuts. And he got loose that other time too, remember? Where was the spell then? Calm down. I suggest we table this discussion entirely until we talk to Marissa. By the way, did she mention if she likes dogs? Maybe we can bring Rusty."

"There is no way I'm bringing that jackass dog to DC; and if you borrow him ever to close a deal, you better not let him get loose. I admit, he's a pain in the neck, but he's my pain in the neck. Anyway, I think you're right, I think I'm over thinking this thing."

"Of course you are, but what the heck, it sounds like a great story to tell; maybe we can tell Marissa, and I'll tell her how I think you should be more respectful of her grandmother. I may ask her if she knows a good dog park in DC, too."

I had to admit, I felt better. Yes, at first I thought maybe there was something to this horoscope nonsense, but Mike made a ton of sense, and I was overthinking everything. These horoscopes were just coincidences; no way they were true. There was absolutely no way this could be tied to that old lady and her fake-ass spells.

We finished our steaks and decided to call it a night since we both had busy work weeks ahead of us. One thing about my friends, which I've always appreciated, is we were pretty tight. I'd do anything for my posse (outside of potential jail items, or job-losing items), and they were the same.

With that, I dropped Mike off, and headed home. I had bigger fish to fry than worrying about horoscopes; that dumb dog had been in the house by himself for a few hours and God knows what he'd been up to. I needed to get home.

***

MONDAY
The All Hands Call

BEEP!!! BEEP!!! BEEP!!! It was 6 AM, and the world's most obnoxious alarm was going off. It was Monday and I was hating life. My body ached from the monsoon calamity of the prior day. In the moment, I hadn't felt too bad. But later that night and now this morning, I felt the hurt.

"Monday, Monday, I hate that day."

I had that song by The Mamas and the Papas in my head and usually I was fired up by it. But, today, I wasn't so sure I had the lyrics right. I couldn't remember; I knew it went something like that, but, honestly, once music got beyond the Rolling Stones, Tom Petty, or Springsteen, I did not have a reliable memory for the words.

I was up and at the sink, brushing away, still singing that dumb "Monday" song, checking for scratches and bruises from the pool debacle. Then some Zeppelin came on the radio and I forgot all about my woes. I could sing along to any Led Zeppelin song. I made sure of that in high school by studying the lyrics, probably did more of that than schoolwork studying. And I knew their tribute bands and the nuances that distinguished one form the other from the real deal. I even went to tribute band shows.

I noticed another scratch on the side of my neck of all places as I toweled off my face, but I had that one show in my mind as "Whole

47

Lotta Love" blared. Back when I'd gone to see Zoso, whose rendition of it was incredible. It was a great show.

I clicked off the radio when the backup alarm went off. I was hopping into my slacks and almost crashed into the dresser, which would have made three days in a row of bizarre debacles. After that dose of Zep, I was feeling much better about the horoscope gobbledygook; there was no way that stuff was real.

So what? My dog ran away? Big deal. That could happen any day. That mutt was always trying to escape and go on joy runs on his own. The pool dealio? Coulda happened to anyone. Besides, how could some hocus pocus words loosen screws? There was no way the Madame snuck over to my parents' house and set everything up, either.

I had my shoes tied when the alarm went off again (the 3rd warning just in case I snoozed twice) and that godforsaken "Monday, Monday" song was back and now stuck in my head. More than those other events, I would have believed the radio to be in on the curse as I shut the darn thing off.

I had to get going. Third alarm meant I was running behind. After firing up my coffee and feeding Rusty, I grabbed the paper for a quick read before I got rolling; and, yes, for the first time in my life, I checked the horoscopes before the sports page.

I flipped open the Washington Post, which I thought was a great paper, and, reluctantly setting the sports section to the side, I found the horoscope for Leo. I was starting not to like the Post, come to think of it, on account of horoscopes. Anyway, there was Leo staring me down so I read it, feeling fearful just a bit:

LEO
*"Don't you worry,
And don't you squirm,
It won't hurt you,
It's only a worm!"*

Ha! That didn't look bad; I was still a little sleepy, but after the last two days' events, it seemed like I was in the clear after all. Unless...I took a moment to consider all the potential bad a worm could bring. The only thing I could see was that worm could be construed to mean snake. I was *not* a snake person; the only kind of snakes I knew were cobra, rattlesnake, and everything else may as well have been the same kind and equally disgusting. I didn't like them. I read the horoscope again. Just a worm. Maybe this horoscope meant nothing, or maybe it meant a tiny snake, regardless, whatever it was, it was not going to hurt me.

I took a quick peak at the other horoscopes and they all seemed normal, look out for love or for work and be open or be closed or friendships cool and family problems come and go, yadda yadda. Same ol same ol, in other words, a bunch of blarney.

I crumpled up the horoscope page and pitched it in the trash.

Now I was feeling good. Time to start my Monday. Breakfast, the sports page, and CNN on in the background was my preferred morning ritual. Get Hyped Monday!

Rusty fed off my mood and he got pumped, which meant he was running around inside and trying to find something inappropriate to chew, so I let him out in the backyard and got myself a bowl of cereal. The week was going to be busy, and a big one for me. It was going to be very important—we had an All Hands Meeting that Monday for which I'd prepared a report last week, and I would likely be called upon to answer questions. We also had some pretty visible projects, so people were counting on me.

One big project was in D.C. at the Norwegian embassy, which was supposed to be gorgeous, and another project in New York City. Believe it or not, we were installing a cell phone antenna in the arm of the Statue of Liberty; it had been in zoning for two years and finally was approved. Due to its location near Battery Park, it was perfect to close out holes in cell coverage in lower Manhattan. We were the first telecom company to ever secure rights to deploy any gear in the statue. I had been working on the teams for both projects and was also responsible for all reporting aspects of each. I was also the go-to on site in case anything went wrong during the installs and launches.

This was a crucial week and I was taking notes on my plans and prepping some statements as I chomped down my corn flakes. Maybe I had some bad luck this weekend when I wasn't paying attention—I messed up with the pool thing screwing too tight, but no big deal, coulda seen it coming if I wasn't in a rush, and, of course, I should have been better prepared with Rusty. I'd been planning for these projects and my role for weeks and I wasn't about to get lazy and unfocused, luck or no luck. Nothing would get the best of me. I was on top of my work game.

My boss told me to be at both locations, and to keep him in the loop on all aspects of the installs. But first, today, we were having an All Hands call to talk about the company's performance last quarter, highlight some items, then talk about these high-profile projects. All I needed to do was make sure a worm didn't bite me. *Haha. Oh, man, Mike was gonna laugh at this one. Sorry girls, and honorable Madamme! Ooooooh, I think I'll be fine.*

I finished up my notes and food, dropped the bowl in the sink and then put Rusty in the basement. I situated his giant dog crate to block him down there—*no funny business today.* I knew many people used these things to put their pets away all day long, but I didn't. Poor guy goes nuts in it; I wasn't sure why because I got him as a rescue dog, but he was usually good when confined to an area of the house when I was out, so I just used it to block him downstairs till I got home at night.

My basement was pretty big, the stuff I left out was "chewable" and the things I didn't want him to mess with (like the remote controls for my tv) were put out of reach. For some reason, he must have not like one of my tall standing lamps, because he'd chewed the lampshade to bits twice. *That* one got put in a closet, and his food & water were near the back door, which had a giant dog door on it, so he could get outside if he needed to. The backyard was fenced in and locked, so he was good to go for the day. No escapes and no shenanigans.

My commute was not long typically (about 20 mins) and had some perks. There were a couple of great straightaways I could rev up my Mustang and accelerate to high speeds, which was fun as heck; but I didn't get too nuts because rush hour traffic—and cops. If I left early enough (which was rare since my cars and dog moved much faster than I did in the morning) I could race a bit more, but usually it was just a straight 20 minutes in moving traffic to get to work.

Apparently, it had rained at some point during the night and at one of the lights I looked over and saw a mashed worm half-way submerged in a low puddle. *Ha. Look out for worms!* After that sighting, I was feeling confident and positive I had been reading into things and acting silly about the horoscopes.

When I got to work, I was feeling good and shot the breeze with some of my colleagues—the usual banter about weekends (I definitely was not going into the horoscopes with anyone; I did tell them Rusty got loose, though, because that was mildly funny and mostly everyone had a dog back at home and could identify) and about going out. Some of us were trying to put a poker game together, but no one was committing yet. Our boss wanted us to get together at 10 AM to talk about the All Hands call and have a mini staff meeting with our division. Piece of cake.

Before I got too involved with my day, I sent Mike a text thanking him for yesterday and also sent him my horoscope, which, of course, he responded to with derision:

"Really? I thought we settled this. Lighten up! It's gonna be a great day. But if it makes you feel better, ping me if things go sideways today."

"You're right; I sent it just in case. I don't know what I was thinking. Delete it."

With that, I jumped into prep for the All Hands Meeting and tuned everyone out.

My morning was broken up by one of my bosses, Greg, who was a good guy, if a bit of a worry wart.

"Billy, can you check that we're good on the Projects Report on the SharePoint site? I want to make sure it's one hundred percent done; we're going to use it for some statuses on the All Hands call later today. I looked at it Friday and it looked ok; I just want one more look at it to make sure we're all set."

"Absolutely, no problem; I'll look right now."

He gave me two thumbs up, which was corny, but at least he meant well. He had a family, and everyone made fun of him for being such a stickler for details, double and triple checking everything all the time. But he got to where he was for a reason, and I made sure to follow his lead. When he was due up for a promotion, he'd be thinking about me and making sure I followed him. As I said, good guy, loyal if you did what he needed, but he never brought along anyone who gave him grief or messed up projects.

They stayed around, and could still be promoted, but, if they were, Greg had nothing to do with it. Once you messed up, you were out in his eyes. But I was killing it with him, and I knew he trusted me.

A quick check of e-mail, and an update on two questions, and then I clicked to the SharePoint site. All was good and where it was supposed to be. The report had a log that showed each region had updated their data, and the spreadsheet was feeding properly, so we were all good.

"Everything's all set; the updates were done and the report is feeding well. It's good, Greg."

"Excellent, thanks again, Billy. You're my go-to guy. We're gonna do really well this quarter."

All I could think was, *you're damn straight we are. Once I kill it at the embassy and in NYC, this will go well toward my annual review and some well-deserved cash.* Man, that was why I liked Mondays. *Get a raise Mondays!* Things were always energetic and promising.

These SharePoint sites were awesome; they were great tools for companies to use to post data that people could update and not have to email all over the place. Case in point, the one we were using for our network buildout plan, we had a ton of information on site, saved to different tabs, for multiple users. Our company built out networks for all the carriers, so we were not married to any one of them, and won contracts from all of them.

The report was built in the following way:

> Tab 1 Was the Summary (rolls up all cell sites per region and by month). This had a summary of progress and tracked the financials as well.
> Tabs 2-6 - Represented each region (North, South, East, & West) & large project (special builds) details.

We had the subcontractors for each region update their tab on Friday mornings of each week, so by Friday COB, the Executive Team could review it. Right now, we were ahead of schedule (thank God), and actually tracking ahead of budget (a bigger thank God). Especially right now, since we had two highly visible projects going to implementation phase this week, which was going to be highlighted on our All Hands call later shortly.

I had a few spare minutes to click around email before our staff meeting. One thing I liked doing was getting work done ASAP and having some moments to myself to make plans and check sports. I messed around a bit then joined the staff meeting.

At our meeting, Greg was outlining how the All Hands call would go. We had a group of four guys reporting to Greg; I was involved with interacting with Operations, and also assisted on ensuring our reporting was caught up.

"Guys, for the call today, we're going to spend the first thirty minutes going over the quarterly results—they were good—and the last half of the call, we are going to review the status of the West Coast cell site build (a multi-carrier one), then spend the last few minutes talking about the embassy prototype build, and then, last, the Statue of Liberty build. Billy, I want you onsite at the embassy and the Statue of Liberty projects assisting with any logistics if need be and letting me know if there are any issues in real time."

"Not a problem; I'm ready."

I actually had never been in an embassy. I heard they're extremely cool, so this was going to be an interesting experience. Regarding the NY trip, I was fired up. I loved New York and was going to be in part of the Statue of Liberty no one got to see, and, time permitting, was planning to visit my cousins in Staten Island.

Usually, All Hands calls were very routine; our CEO gave financial results, hopefully nothing too chaotic (like mergers or sales of the company), and we all went our merry way. This one was a bit different because we were going to review in detail some of the projects I was going to be on site for.

The call was set for 2PM Eastern so everyone could join in, since our company had around 1200 people across multiple time zones, and that meant fifteen minutes early to ensure Skype meeting functionality.

After lunch, around 1:30 PM, I prepped myself for the call just in case I was asked to speak. Sometimes the CEO fired off questions, particularly to leads on major projects. I brushed up on details and then checked emails for last minute changes or notifications. Everything was fine and my spreadsheets were all set up and functioning. I had a few minutes to kill and I wanted to go into the call feeling relaxed.

Work permits us our short breaks at the computer, so I opened up YouTube to watch some videos. One of my favorite things to watch was stunt video footage—particularly stunt fails. Out of the many stuntmen in the world, I totally loved Evel Knievel; he was the best. I pulled up his Snake River jump when he went airborne in some makeshift rocket.

That jump was amazing, and it was terrifying and tragic when the rocket crashed. I watched the video a few times and then a few other Knievel videos—great guy and totally crazy, but brave. I had a few minutes left before the meeting, so I opened up my Hotmail account to check on an Amazon order on a book called *Doing More by Working Less*. I wasn't paying much attention, just opening some emails, until I got to the one that I thought was the order confirmation. When I opened it, a window popped up on my screen with a warning sign and then I heard, "Your account and personal information may have been accessed, please contact Spyware Solutions for a free evaluation." I sat frozen for a second not sure what to do because the mouse was frozen. The message began to repeat itself and seemed to be getting louder, so I quickly shut down the computer. *I don't believe it, and I don't have time for this; I need to get on the call. It's 1:50. Can't be late. I'll restart the computer and jump on the call early.*

I powered on the computer and everything was normal. Those stupid prize popups happened every so often and they were a nuisance. Usually you could just click out of them or turn the computer off and fire it back up and, bingo, everything was fine. And everything was. I opened Skype and waited.

At 1:55, Elizabeth our CEO's Executive Admin chimed in:

"Hi everyone, this is Elizabeth Anderson, Tom Duncan's admin; please make sure all your devices are on mute, for the call. The agenda is 45 minutes of presentations by the Executive Teams and 15 minutes for any questions."

Our CEO was a great guy; Tom Duncan ran the company well, was fair, and liked to have fun, too. Our company had done pretty well, and one thing they did was share things when possible. When the company hit our financial goals, I received a defined bonus plan, *and* we had parties, which was unusual in today's environment. Each office (there were eight) had an annual Holiday Party on site and catered (nothing nuts, but some good food and alcohol and each employee got two tickets free). We had annual "Spring Flings" in our parking lot and the field next to our building, which became a giant cookout: burgers, dogs, brats, and trash cans full of beers and sodas or water. We'd had bands play these events, too. Again, it all started at the top, and Tom was that type of guy—he made work fun. One time we held a party in the office that had different themes for different floors (an Italian floor, a Tex-Mex floor, a Cowboy floor, a French floor); everyone on their floor contributed to the catering or just helped on the logistics. And yes, more trash cans with beer and other things. All good and fun. So, the All Hands calls were welcome and well run.

At 2:00, Tom chimed in, "Hi everyone, welcome to our Quarterly Call. We're going to go over the 1st Q results, talk about some bigger projects, then open the floor to questions. *Please* remember the only dumb questions are whether the Annual Party will be at Disney World. We keep getting that one on the anonymous e-mail box question, and one day I might have IT try to figure out who keeps sending it. We had a great quarter, but not *that* great. And to the Disney fan out there: touché for asking every call—I like the moxie and wish we could go. And maybe swing by Gatorland, conveniently close to Disney, and feed you to some gators."

Again, he was fun. And in no way was I the one asking about Disney; I knew better to mess around with that stuff. But that Gatorland thing sounded like fun! *I may have to check that out sometime. I bet old Knievel would have loved to jump over a croc pit.*

"Our first quarter results were great; we're ahead of our revenue goals, and expenses are right on line. Jeff, our CFO, will give us a quick run down."

Jeff Shipp, the CFO, went through his slides, all of which showed what our CEO had just said; it all looked good.

Next, our VP of Sales, Marie Spanos, rolled through her data, and ended with, "We are really excited about our government accounts; we have an embassy trial we're going to complete tomorrow, and had crews all week at the Statue of Liberty in New York. Our wireless ethernet product is much easier to get through zoning at these high-profile locations, so we believe we can pursue more of them."

Then the call was turned over to John Bankton, our Network Delivery VP, to discuss the Operations build status.

"Good afternoon everyone, we'll get to the Network Build portion now as I open our status reports."

He went through the 1st tab, the summary tab. John was a good guy, if but a tad monotone. I tended to zone out when he spoke, which I did this time around, too, thinking about Zoso and feeling like a million bucks because my dad had let me take out his prized car for the evening.

When I checked back in, John was still going.

"Everyone has heard the embassy project gets turned up tomorrow, and later this week, the Statue of Liberty does, too. Let's look at the regions."

And he opened that tab, from the West.

"You can see Los Angeles, and Orange County doing well."

And then, the screen blinked for a second and froze.

"We'll take a look at Seattle; just a minute as soon as my screen unfreezes. Can everyone see this?"

It was not unusual for calls with a gazillion users to freeze up. And John had a rep for being clunky with the buttons. The freeze went on for longer than usual and I had a strange inkling in the back of my mind, but I was refocusing and eager to hear about results despite enjoying that Zeppelin song from this morning which popped into my head.

We were all still looking at Southern California, when a clearly audible voice came through the speakers:

"It is possible your account has a malware product on it; your information may be at risk."

Then the call took an abrupt change; instead of seeing an excel spreadsheet with lines of data, it moved...to You Tube. A video of ABC's Wild World of Sports.

"Hello everyone, this is John again. We're not sure why, but the screen has locked onto YouTube instead of our SharePoint site; we're attempting to disengage it. Please hold on."

Uh oh. YouTube? Somebody's gonna get busted if they're goofing off on YouTube during this All Hands call; I knew a couple of the guys in the IT group, and I hoped it was not them. They were cool guys and had always helped me. But I was getting worried. That stupid warning had happened to me earlier...

And then we saw the first item—Evel Knievel, talking to Howard Cosell, and then getting on his bike to run down a ramp for a quick jump over several buses. One of the same clips I had just seen before the call. *Oh no...* Then Evel ran through several more jumps and crashes; the same ones I had just seen! Normally, I would have been enjoying this little bit of chaos, but not with 1,200 of my closest friends, including the CEO, the CFO, and everyone else who had the power to fire me all seeing the same videos that I had just watched!

Good God! My BS is what's disrupting the call. I hoped my good friends in IT would fix it quick! Or, more importantly, that they couldn't trace this thing to me!

"We're still stuck, everyone, and will disconnect the call. Thanks for your patience."

Except nothing disconnected; for the next 15 minutes, Evel jumped over a number of things: buses, the pool with the sharks, and even that rocket ship over Snake River, including several crashes where he wiped out. I tried disconnecting but couldn't. All the people around me, too, were trying to disconnect, but couldn't. Some were laughing with the crashes, and no one was terribly concerned, until my boss came out and said, "Guys, I just got a text message from the CFO; somehow a virus or worm came through the SharePoint site and is erasing all of our transactions. All of it. Payroll, taxes, bills we pay. IT has no idea how it's on our network, but all managers have been told to tell everyone verbally to turn everything off immediately! And the entire IT Department is going to be combing through every transaction to see how it was loaded onto our network. Tom said if someone was goofing off and downloaded something stupid or went to a site they shouldn't be on and caused this, that guy is getting fired. They are looking at everyone's email accounts who had anything to do with the SharePoint report. That means us, too."

*No way, this can't be...*I thought about my morning horoscope:

> ## *"Don't you worry,*
> ## *And don't you squirm,*
> ## *It won't hurt you,*
> ## *It's only a worm!"*

Good God, no. I need this gig. All I had done was check my Hotmail account and watched one Evel Knievel jump. Well, maybe a couple of Evel jumps. But that was nothing I hadn't done before. Just some innocent YouTubing...

Anyway, our entire company was offline, and our IT Department was working feverishly to figure out how Evel Knievel and YouTube were somehow erasing all our records. And they were equally feverishly working to see who touched the SharePoint Report and may have caused it. Thank God they didn't know who Madame Pearl was, what the Leo horoscope for today said, and if I knew why any of this could happen.

Just then, my boss, Greg, was standing over me looking perplexed and stressed.

"Billy, is there anything I need to know about this? Did you notice anything with the report when you looked at it this morning, or last week?"

"Absolutely not. That thing worked perfectly; I thought it looked like it did every other time I opened it. I didn't notice it work faster or slower, or anything. Just like normal."

"The VP of IT is texting everyone to ask any staff if they have anything they want to tell us that might help. The worm just erased all of our previous two year's financial records, and they have a firewall with twenty-two layers of protection for this year's, but six of them are gone. Once the worm gets through them, it will access that data, and it's not backed up."

If only this worm stuck to broadcasting Evel's crashes. *This is bad.* Data that was not backed up, and IT people looking at us all. I decided my only course of action was to say, "I hope those guys catch the hacker; I have no idea if I can help but will if they think I can."

I had no idea if Madame Pearl's thing was behind this; I didn't do dumb stuff on e-mails or websites, at least not by reputation, so I decided to lay low. The worst thing they could do was trace it to me and can me. I was a waiter once; I could do it again. I enjoyed my time in the food services industry, and, by the looks of everything, I may have to again. This time, I would go to Italian places; I had always enjoyed Italian food the best. Maybe I'd actually learn to cook something.

"Legal is saying if an employee did this by going on websites prohibited by the policy, they may be liable."

"I hope they catch the hacker, and I hope, if it's an employee, it turns out to be an accident; nobody meant for this to happen, I'm sure."

Just then another text to Greg's cell phone.

"They just said to keep everything shut off. They are going to try an 'Eco-Purge.' It sounds like some kind of electronic flame thrower."

I secretly hoped they could let me take that flame thrower to my computer first, leave it a melted mess. In that moment, I had a fantasy of "accidentally" knocking the whole thing on to the ground. *Would that be suspicious?*

Christ, I was getting nervous. Pearl was real and coming after me! It was happening, and not going away. Getting nervous? Getting nervous was well gone and in the rear-view mirror; I needed a lifeline. I sent Mike a quick text.

"Dude, are you there? I really need to talk to you."

Immediately he shot back:

"Did you get her number for me? That is extremely cool of you; send it. Better yet, send it and let's go to lunch there today if we can."

"No, I don't have her number, I don't know if I can get it. I have a serious thing at work here and need to talk to you."

"OK, call me."

I stepped outside to make the call and told him we had some type of IT meltdown during our All Hands call, and right now it was replaying all kinds of crap that had been on my computer screen twenty minutes before the call, and it was now destroying the company's financial records. Then I got to the part about IT calling it a virus or a *"worm"* and that they were now trying to stop it and discover the culprit, which meant they would be tracking back to me!

"What makes you think it's because of you?"

"Because I was looking at Evel Knievel jump all kinds of crap, crash all over the place, and now it's on every computer in the company. The same stuff that I was literally looking at is now stuck on everyone's screens, *and* the IT Group is calling this a "worm"!

"OK, so IT viruses happen all the time, why are you freaking out?"

"Because my horoscope said to look out for worms! Worms, Dammit!!"

"Not again with this. Man, are you a pansy? When this thing blows over, I'm taking you to go buy a sun dress and make you start wearing it. Wait till I tell Marissa. This will only enhance my chances with her— she'll see you for the dope you are."

"Oh yeah? Well listen to this:

"Don't you worry,
And don't you squirm,
It won't hurt you,
It's only a worm!"

"Dude, it's only a poem, a really bad one, I might add, and maybe you should be on the lookout when you're gardening. Which I imagine you feel at home in, since you're a pansy."

It was times like this that the support from my friends (my best friend in particular) that reminded me friendship was priceless. I was so fortunate.

"I think I'm gonna tell my boss. Maybe they can look at my computer, trace something, and stop it."

"Are you nuts? Let's just say they did that, and find your Evel Knievel crap, what are you gonna tell them? Some old lady drilled you with a curse? You'll be locked up alright, but not in jail. Please, please, do not do this. Lay low; you told me the IT guys are on it, right? Let them do their jobs. I'm your best friend, if you ever do anything for me, *please* do this. Lay low, let them, do their thing."

"OK, I will. I'll say a quick prayer, maybe add to the good stuff I promised I'd do when chasing that stupid dog all over the place. I don't know what I did to deserve this, but I do not deserve this stress. I'm laying low for now."

"No, not any of that 'for now' stuff; you lay low, stay laid low, or I'm telling your parents how their station wagon ended up in your neighbor's backyard, and who snuck their booze to the cabin. I took the heat for both of those debacles in high school but will sing like a canary if you don't lay low now. Trust me."

Again, I was humbled at the level of kindness and support my friends gave me in my times of need. I was truly blessed. With support like this, how could I not take such sage advice.

"Alright, alright; I'll lay low."

"That's my boy. Now, don't screw this up. I don't want a depressed, unemployed friend to have to lend money to. Besides, first things that happen is that you sell the car and the dog. I can't take over your car payment and sure as heck don't like dogs. And let's try to reconvene later today…and for God's sake, don't tell anyone this is some curse. I have a hard-enough time when I tell people we still hang. It'll be twice as hard if you're in a straitjacket, mumbling about curses and old ladies etc."

Mike and I hung up and I had renewed energy to stay the course and play things out. When I returned to the floor, Greg was telling everyone the CEO apparently tried turning on his computer, and it was still stuck on Evel—the time he crashed into the fountains at Vegas. The only silver lining in this cloud was our CEO rides a Harley to work and actually loved Evel Knievel. Maybe this crisis would have a happy ending. Maybe that eco/flame throwing IT super move would work. Maybe this investigation would end with us blaming Russian hackers. Maybe the Powerball ticket in my pocket was actually going to pay out for once.

While I decided to listen to Mike's advice on what to do, I was having trouble getting on board with the happenstance theory. If it hadn't been my videos or they hadn't mentioned the "worm" idea, then I'd be in the clear with the curse. But it was just too coincidental. And yet, *how can I believe this trash?*

Greg was on the phone and talking to all of us at our desks, saying, "Anyway, I know you work hard and not doing dumb stuff on the computer; hopefully IT can figure it out. I do know we are supposed to have backups."

"Yeah, maybe this will stop," someone chimed in, trying to stay positive.

I was glad they offered that because I was worried I'd confess. For a second, I thought maybe I should tell Greg about this Madame Pearl thing, but Mike's asshole voice chimed in and told me to "lay low, dummy."

I could not confess—at least not yet. Besides, I didn't do anything on purpose. *Lay low, dummy*. I decided to continue staying the course.

Another text, this one from corporate. "Apparently the worm has been spotted on AT&Ts and Verizon's networks, too, affecting the cell sites we have built for them. They are both contacting us to see if a 'data erasing virus/worm' is affecting us. Cell phone coverage for the state of Washington just stopped."

The hits kept on coming.

Greg called over to us, "You folks see the text?"

"Yes, hopefully they have good IT departments, too," someone shot back.

I decided to keep my theories to myself. *Lay low and hope IT fixes it.*

A little while later, Greg came on to the floor with a grim and defeated look on his face. "Well, guys, we may as well head home. Don't anyone worry, I once remember an AT&T outage that took down the entire Northeast for a few hours; they'll fix it. Billy, I'll text you tonight about the embassy stuff. The CEO said via another text, we're still going unless this somehow could affect it. He doesn't want to spook them out of the job. I'll text you tonight regardless."

Getting out of there was welcome news, although nothing had been solved. I was still worried, but if I got fired, I'd rather get the call while at home with my dog than in front of everyone at the office. So, I packed up all of my things, made sure I didn't leave anything out (like my dumb newspaper which had been opened to the horoscopes, but even my photos, stationary, and coffee mugs) and headed out.

I'm not sure if I even wanted to go near the embassy tomorrow. I didn't know what I could do to stop this thing; maybe when I got downtown tomorrow, I could swing by Madame Pearl's and let her know I totally was sorry if I offended her. Who knows, maybe I could fix something for her, or maybe just beg my way out of this. This was three days in a row of things that looked more and more like they were tied to my Friday night curse!

Anyway, I got home at 3 PM, and turned on CNN only to find the reporter saying, "Hello everyone; no one has solved this unusual e-mail virus or worm, but cell phone coverage in the Pacific Northwest is currently out. AT&T and Verizon have no comment at this time other than to say their spyware partners are actively working on the trace and believe they will have service restored later this evening. They believe it originated from the East Coast."

Good Lord, maybe, maybe, maybe this will fix itself? I decided I was not watching anymore tv the rest of the night, except maybe Netflix.

After several hours of Netflix, I received a text from my boss at 10 PM.

"Billy! Great news. It's fixed!! We're on for tomorrow. Ping me when you get there and keep me in the loop on things. The only thing IT was unhappy about was when they purged everything, they torched all records associated with the SharePoint site, so now they can't tell how the virus actually happened. Thanks for all— Greg."

Holy shit! The best news of my life! Mike was right. I was happy he was, though now I figured I'd have to pay for his lunch and, while I wasn't sad about the curse being fixed, I did feel weird about it not being true. Part of me almost wanted it to be true, if for no other reason than to be right and Mike wrong, which then meant I was wrong about my earlier proposition that curses were fake. This was all crazy and a nightmare. I reached over and gave Rusty a good scratch behind the ears and then, of course, he tricked me into a lengthy belly rub. Then I texted back.

"They can't? That's too bad. Well at least they fixed it. Thanks for the update, I'll head to DC in the morning and be onsite at the embassy by 8:30 AM. Thx for all—Billy."

Thank God, I thought, our short-term national nightmare was over, or at least my short-term national nightmare was over. Even CNN was in a better mood, as they were saying that AT&T and Verizon's networks were back. Apparently that electronic flame throwing super move our IT Group performed actually worked, and just in time. They were down to the last two firewalls when it took effect. Everything was working now, and we were green-lighted for tomorrow at the embassy. I wondered what tomorrow's horoscope would have in store for me.

At an embassy! I can hardly wait!

I didn't know how, but I needed to get to Madame Pearl and beg forgiveness, or something. I needed this curse or bad luck or worm or whatever it was to stop. I was generally a lucky person, but this was like playing blackjack with the Devil and loaded decks; my luck was running out. Rusty and the wedding cake was starting to look like Christmas morning compared to today's debacle. Anyway, at least I made it through another day. With any luck I could get to Madame Pearl in the morning and do my best to stay off the news. I ended my day with a quick text to my stalwart wingman Mike, who once again proved why my posse is the best.

"I told you, dummy, 'Operation Lay Low' was the way to go. Now let's just chalk this thing up to some bad luck, a weird coincidence, and stop making noises about curses. You're in DC tomorrow right? That embassy job? Good. I'll try to come down, too, and maybe we swing by Marissa's restaurant for lunch or drinks."

"Alright; thanks again for listening, I really appreciate it."

Mike was right and now everything was fixed. All I had to do was get a good night's sleep and make sure no chaos happened the rest of the week. Then, I'd be a hero and maybe even hanging with Mike more than usual would help me meet someone. *Yeah, you're not that lucky,* I told myself. Maybe not, but things were good now, anyway. I was sure more good was to come.

***

TUESDAY
The Embassy

The events of the last few days made me a bit more nervous when I reached for my newspaper Tuesday morning. I was hoping Monday had just been a bump in the road (Mondays usually are, right?) My week could only get better. I still didn't know if I believed my horoscopes were coming true, but I decided to see what Tuesday had in store since I'd had my coffee and morning does of the sports section:

LEO
"Today's the Day for sparkles
That go high and show much light,
For today you'll be the center,
Of a story which shines bright!
Enjoy!"

I had no idea what that could mean, and, frankly, I didn't care what happened to me that day; after an e-mail virus/worm that somehow shut down thirty-five million cellphones (allegedly, I might add, in case the statute of limitations has not run out), the day's events couldn't be that bad. In fact, I considered the previous day a gigantic bullet dodged, and the next day, I was playing with "house money," something I rarely do, since when I gamble at casinos, I usually have lost all of my money by the end of the day.

Alright, again I didn't care what happened, considering yesterday, the implications, and thank God a great ending. I couldn't ponder my fate for long, however, because I had to haul ass to DC by 8:30 AM and wasn't a morning person. In short, I needed a jet in the Mustang to be on time.

Rusty was secured in the basement so I grabbed my bag and fired up the 'stang; at least the day would start as any good day should, with the Rolling Stones loud in my car as I rolled onto the street, and the weather was great and very conducive for driving…fast.

If "Street Fighting Man" by the Rolling Stones didn't get your pulse going, nothing would; and it came on just as I entered the Dulles Toll Road, which was the fastest way to Washington DC in the morning. Like every other way to Washington DC in the morning, the dang road was jammed with God knows how many cars.

Anyway, I needed to be at the Norwegian embassy at 8:30 to see the final touches of what our company had installed: new wave wireless repeaters, or in layman's terms, bad ass cell phone hot spots. These things had been in development for years, and what they were best at was compressing and encrypting digital voice and data signals for phones, internet, and video. Wirelessly.

All these repeaters needed was some power; they could be picked up and moved anywhere in the building and they would amplify the signal up to five times the normal strength. What made these models particularly good was they were capable of transmitting through cement up to four feet thick. One thing I had found out about embassies was not only were they gorgeous inside and out, they were built like forts. Walls that were loaded with insulation and cement, and very thick; the kind of stuff that slowed down or blocked signals.

These repeaters were small and could be plugged in outlets after a dish was installed on the roof, and another one in the basement; between them, the ones plugged in on each floor literally made the signals hyper strong. Today, we were going to be testing the strength between the dishes and the "plug-ins" on each floor.

The thing that our CEO was most fired up about (which of course made everyone equally fired up or nervous) is if this went well, it could lead to a contract for all the embassies in Washington DC, which is something like one hundred-fifty locations. A boon for sure. With yesterday's events well under control, our plan was to not adjust the schedule at all, and to go full speed ahead while tech worked overtime to patch up the damage of the worm.

For this install, we had our best contractor, Lightwalkers, based out of Florida, to do the job. I had worked with them for years. The President of the company, Cam Matlack, was great and had never let me down. He once worked at risk of not getting paid for one of my previous telco companies that eventually went into vapor due to a merger; But I got him paid in the end, and we'd been fantastic partners ever since. He was great and never let me down, which was why he had this job—he'd personally been on site several times a week for the last six weeks, ensuring all wiring was flawless, and pressure testing circuit strength throughout the last two weeks.

That morning, we had to run through a series of tests in preparation for a full-blown demonstration for the Ambassador of Norway and several members of Congress later in the evening. Also in attendance were several VPs from my company (Operations, and Sales), and, of course, our CEO. If I pulled this off in front of our top brass and the embassy's leadership and special guests, I'd be the golden boy, set for a raise and other big things. This could not go badly.

Getting to DC went much easier than I thought. I arrived in Washington around 8:10, just over the Key Bridge, and was poised to cross into Georgetown. At the light, I couldn't help but think of the Exorcist stairs; the scene where the priest flew out of the window was all filmed right there, just one hundred yards to the left of where I was. I always marveled at that and thought it was very cool and a must see. Two minutes is all it took, and it was very, very cool. As traffic rolled back to life, I thought I would take my next date to the steps and impress them with my film trivia.

Anyway, I wasn't looking for an exorcism that morning, (maybe I should have been, considering recent events), so I made a right and headed down M Street into the heart of the city. My plan was, per GPS, to get to Wisconsin Avenue, make a left onto it, and head about five miles down till I ran into Massachusetts Avenue, where the embassy was. GPS had me there a few minutes early and I would still be able to see some of the great buildings in Georgetown.

As I pulled up to the embassy, I saw Cam's Lightwalkers logo on three work vans parked down a side street, so I was relieved they'd arrived on time. Once I parked, I circled around front, checked in through the secured entrance (metal detectors, and a wand), picked up my badge, and was good to go.

Now, I had to admit, I had never been in any embassy before, and I was sure they were all impressive, but this one was unreal. It had four floors, three elevators, marble and mahogany wood carvings everywhere. It literally looked like what I'd imagine a castle would look like; the main staircase must've been fifteen feet wide, entirely made of what looked like marble, and looked solid as a fort. And gorgeous.

The main foyer had a ceiling that went to the second floor, and that must've been thirty feet high. I had to think that the heating bill in this place must have been a fortune! But, judging by the looks of the secretaries and attaches and other employees dressed comfortably, I guessed it could be comfortable. Besides, in the several parlor rooms on the first floor, each had an enormous fireplace which was functional, so keeping warm was probably not a problem. The two top floors were the ambassador's residence and private office; rarely did contractors go there, although we would, with escorts, of course.

After I'd taken in the impressive foyer, I spotted Cam speaking with a crewman and a security guard. He shook each hand and waved me over and I got a quick status review: both dishes were installed, there were over seventy outlets in the house, we installed twenty-four repeaters (six on each floor), testing commenced floor by floor at 10 AM, and a walk through would be at 2 PM for my company's senior staff, at 5:30, the doors would open and guests begin arriving for a cocktail hour, at 6 PM the ambassador would give a short speech, followed by a member of Congress, then our CEO at 6:30 PM, we'd have a demonstration manned by our CEO at 8:30, and all would be wrapped up.

"So far so good," Cam insisted.

The dishes had been installed, and initial tests looked great. These devices were Tonka toy tough; each repeater was confined in a hard steel box, with a thick rubber coating and the large ones on the roof and in the basement the size of a microwave oven and were as strong as Fort Knox.

Both were hard wired into the electrical system of the building, and transmitted the signal on the same copper that carried the electricity. By having plug in devices (small by the way) into outlets, the signal was forwarded to wireless devices throughout the building. And it worked really well. Nearly T-1 speeds via wireless! Our company was doing great things and I was next in line for a big promotion. That is, if all went well.

So there we were, it was 10 AM and it was time to start testing things. One thing about Cam and his Lightwalkers was they knew how important this project was to us. It was a high-profile project which would likely lead to a huge revenue stream, and was going to put our company into an envious position: we were the government's provider of choice for this sensitive project. Not only did it need to be secure, but it needed to work, and not embarrass anyone. The Lightwalkers brought twelve technicians, (three for each floor), and installed a temporary NOC (Network Operations Center) in the basement, and also installed monitoring equipment complete with video in three telco closets to ensure the system was best managed, guarded, and equipped for any issues.

We planned to start from the basement floor, test the signal strength and power for each of the seventy plug-in repeaters, as well as the two dishes.

"Billy, we're ready to start the sweep. Heading to the basement." Cam's voice came to me loud and clear on a private network walkie talkie device.

"Sounds good, let me know once we actually start."

And the basement checked out flawlessly; all fourteen devices were well into the green, and the dish in the basement was reading well above parameters.

"All good on L1, heading to the main floor."

And on and on this went. We went floor by floor, and everything looked good. The only glitch was a readout on the third floor for a weak zone. And that turned out to be a false alarm; the plug-in device on that floor didn't engage it's locking mechanism once installed. It correctly read out to the system a weaker signal, which we recognized. By going to it, we troubleshot it in literally thirty seconds and swapped it out for a better locking device. From a network performance perspective, it probably wouldn't have even registered due to each floor having robust coverage. But from a compliance perspective it was great; we knew the coverage was weak due to the feedback from the device and we were able to replace it before a service issue surfaced. The embassy's IT Officer was with us and was equally impressed.

"Guys, I'm not thrilled we had an equipment issue, but I am glad we caught it during routine checks; this further shows we made a good decision going with your firm for this."

At 1PM, the system was fully tested and good to go. We were ready for our Senior Staff test and walk-through. Our VP of Sales, Marie Spanos, was on hand and at the podium, the same podium the ambassador, a congressman, and our CEO would later address the crowd from tonight during the live test.

"Billy, we're ready. Please engage the monitors and let's get ready for real tests," said Cam.

On the main floor, we had two enormous 75-inch big screen

monitors flanking the podium, and, throughout the amphitheater, we had a 45-inch screen deployed every eight feet. All told, we had sixteen screens (including the 75-inchers), and there was no question this would be visible to everyone on the main floor. Also, not to sell the other floors short, each one had an additional eight 45-inch screens deployed on the walls—this included the three in the ambassador's private residence, one of which was in his bedroom. This embassy looked like it had more monitors than a NASA launch room. And it was all working flawlessly.

"Monitors all engaged, showing green everywhere," Cam relayed to me, as I stood next to Marie so she heard as well.

"Great, let's start the first test."

And it was a beautiful one. Since this was a technological play, we went with that theme; a space shuttle taking off in panoramic view, on every screen in the building. sixty-four in total, and not an ounce of signal loss on any.

"Absolutely looking good on the main floor!"

"All good on the Basement."

"Three's a charm on the third…"

"As is four. All good."

"Ambassador's private monitors running great."

And so on, and so on. We had the shuttle flight and a NASCAR driving interactive chase test, both of which accessed our company's email server (I was still nervous considering yesterday), but all went well. The thing was running marvelously.

"Go for a Google search test," I said in effort to try everything. And that worked as well.

By 3 PM, we had run through the battery of tests and this was rolling very well. Even our VP of Sales, who was the skeptic of skeptics, relaxed.

"Billy, your team and that contractor have done a great job; we're ready."

"Thanks Marie, I think we are too. I'll relax at 9PM when all is done."

We had an hour before the cocktail start. One thing I had been unaware of (but was now looking forward to) was that the event, beginning with the cocktail hour, was getting some really good local news coverage. NBC Channel 4 was sending its highest-followed correspondent, Connie Fitzgerald, to cover the proceedings, and it was a good thing she got there at 4 PM instead of 2 PM, or we might not have finished the testing. Not only was she a great reporter, she looked like a supermodel, and Cam's team was starting to congregate around her crew.

"Do you guys need any help setting up? We have twelve techs on site and know the power of this building inside and out."

"No thanks. Our units run entirely on batteries, so we don't have to worry about this."

"Any uplink concerns? We have gear that can measure all of it."

"Thanks, but we already confirmed we are at one hundred and ten percent capacity and are good."

I had to admit, even I got in the mix.

"Guys, Cam asked me to find you for a last briefing; also, Miss Fitzgerald, I was going to that Starbucks next door for a quick coffee before we roll, do you want anything?"

"No, thank you, but I appreciate the offer. We're good."

And so it went; one helpful knucklehead after another, offering everything under the sun except to jumpstart her car. Thank God Cam got there, reeled his crew in and got them to the basement for a last review.

At 4:30 I received a text from Mike.

"Hey, is it cool if I come down there and see the demo, too? Afterwards, we can go grab dinner if you want; maybe drinks. I've never been to an embassy."

"Of course; try to be here no later than 6:00. That's when it's 'showtime'. And everything looks great so far; even my horoscope had some uplifting thing about how I'll be a shining sparkly star or something. Maybe if this curse is real, Madame Pearl threw me a bone."

"Whatever, dude; are there any hotties there or what?"

"The news chick is smoking hot, but everybody's helping her so much it's like she has her own Secret Service detail. But it's the Norwegian embassy, the rest of the staff is very attractive."

"Outstanding, see you at six."

"Perfect; I'll put your name on the list and see you when you get here."

We still had some items to prep for, but this thing was humming along and I felt great where we were; the schedule was running right on time:

5:15—the sponsoring congressman, Jim Andrews from Maryland, walked in with Ambassador Georth (of Norway), and his wife, Mrs. Georth. The ambassador and his wife both looked as if they were part of a Royal family. Regal, distinguished, all of the above. The congressman looked like a congressman; sharp dressed, well portrayed, and in his element. Lightwalkers was based out of Maryland, and he had personally recommended them. We were all set. Our CEO Tom Duncan also arrived and was beaming seeing how everything looked great.

5:30—the Happy Hour started. There were probably two hundred people in the great room, and it was hard to keep track of anyone. Except for the News 4 reporter who was roving throughout the crowd interviewing people, and who had just as many eyes roving on her. Being a people watcher, I got a kick catching somebody getting busted checking out someone they shouldn't. I saw no less than four wives elbow, who I can assume were, their husbands for staring too long. Even the ambassador was uncharacteristically available for an impromptu interview.

"We are glad to be the first test of this newfound technology; Norway is working to be at the cutting edge."

And so on, and so on. The ambassador went on and on, babbling about this and that seemingly to keep the audience of Connie. For minutes I watched. Then he disappeared into the crowd.

Just then, I saw Mike from across the room; he waved, then went back to talking to one of the Embassy staff's welcome committee, who was extremely attractive. *Surprise, surprise. Oh well, I have work to do.* I couldn't get wrapped up in talking to women when my future and potential raise was on the line!

Soon the Happy Hour was in full swing, complete with music and food and everyone having a good time. The news crew set up their cameras to record the event, and interviews were over. It was nearly 6PM, which meant speeches. Then it was showtime. I was not drinking a drop, and Cam and I were in constant communication via text and our walkie talkies when we could hear. Everyone else could enjoy the party; we were here to make sure it worked.

At 5:55, the ambassador's press secretary took to the podium to reel in the crowd.

"Ladies and Gentlemen; Ladies and Gentlemen. May I have your attention, please?"

The crowd quieted down.

"Please meet the Ambassador of Norway, the honorable Whitaker Georth!"

The crowd gave a rousing round of applause. The combination of Connie's appearance and the open bar fueled the applause.

I will admit, however, the ambassador could give a great speech. He went through the details of how this technology was installed by both Norway and several IT companies and it really was a team effort, and how it would lead to faster communications in a secure environment, and it was good for both countries.

Then he turned it over to Congressman Andrews, who gave an equally good speech, who then introduced my CEO, who thanked everyone for giving us the opportunity to be part of the team, then asked out loud, "Are you guys ready to see our technology in action?"

A resounding "YEEESSS!" broke out nearly in unison.

"All right, let's fire this thing up!"

There was another loud round of applause, and off we went. First, through the space shuttle launch, a view of a docking to the International Space Station, then onto NASCAR.

"Anyone want to see what it's like to win the Daytona 500? From inside a car? We're going to turn on the interactive link!"

"YEEESSS!!"

And then we were in a little-known recording of Richard Petty winning the 1974 Daytona 500 in his bad ass Dodge Charger; right in the cockpit. Powered of course, by perhaps the greatest engine of all time: the 426 Hemi. All from inside the King's cockpit, He has always been the coolest driver ever in NASCAR. No wonder he's called The King.

"How's it going Richard, we have Yarborough closing on you."

"My horses are going strong, I've got a lot left; give me a head's up when he's within two car lengths and I'll drop the hammer."

"He's there now, and we're on the final lap; drop it!"

This was too cool; we felt like we were inside the King's car as he jetted around that final lap in that beautiful Charger.

Just as the King lit it up, and he approached the finish line; I saw a small flash on the left 75-inch monitor, followed by an even larger flash on the right side one. Then all at once, all sixty-four monitors, on four floors, blasted out of there frames in a sparkle show that would have made any 4th of July event proud. I didn't know if I should cry, or be impressed that it happened in sync, all at the exact same time.

If it wasn't enough to have the sparks (soon to be followed by flames), you could still hear the whine of Petty's race car roaring to life as he and his crew were whooping it up. Almost as if they were celebrating this debacle (and my career) going up in sparks and flames. Loudly, too, I might add.

But that soon stopped as the speaker wires melted under the hail of sparks. The lights in the embassy then went out, only to be replaced by emergency lights and alarms. The only thing that might have been more horrible to see then sixty-four monitors explode, was the face of my CEO, who's head looked like it was going to explode as he glared at me from across the room. *Thank God for distance and witnesses.*

Another look I caught was from Mike, who had a look of "I'm out of here," as he quickly bolted holding hands and dragging along one of the young ladies he was talking to at the beginning of the party now debacle.

Yes, it was approaching "Every Man for Himself" time; unfortunately for me, I had no such luxury. I was stuck on board and had to see this thing to the bitter, bitter end. I was staying.

Smoke was all over the place and people started for the emergency exits; then it happened. Sprinklers. Everywhere. I felt like I had gone from a horrific cookout that went bad (the smoke was thick but not that bad, and the sparks stopped when the power was cut by Cam), to the "Perfect Storm." Water. Everywhere. And I mean everywhere. Norway must have the most advanced sprinklers in the world. Everything was getting soaked. Including the two priceless Munch paintings they had flanking their enormous fireplace. Munch was Norway's most famous painter whose work called "Scream" was the inspiration for the mask worn by the killers in the movie "Scream". And boy did I feel like making that same face and letting out a howl. My whole team did, and I didn't dare look back at the CEO in that moment.

I saw the look of anguish on the ambassador's face as he looked at the paintings from across the room, so I dashed over and grabbed them off the wall and put them under a tarp covering Cam's tools.

At least those won't get ruined; quite unlike my career, which just exploded with sixty-four giant tv sets.

And the reporter? I overheard her asking her crew, "Did you guys catch that? Please tell me you did."

I was a fan of hers until that; I didn't care how hot she was. This event needed no recordings of any kind.

It took about twenty minutes for everyone to safely exit, and by then the DC Fire Department was on site, going room to room to make sure there was no danger.

"Ambassador, the facility is secure; we are convinced that once the power was cut it eliminated any chance for fire. That and the fantastic response of that sprinkler system, really soaked everything. In fact, I have never seen a system like that deployed, how does it work?"

"It's a double banked system; first is sprays water from jets, then goes into 'mist mode;' deploying a mist thicker than any fog on the planet. It will soak anything in three inches of water that is not fully covered. The only silver lining of this mess is, that young man (he was pointing to me) covered our two priceless Munch paintings before they were ruined. They are literally priceless. I am, however, not pleased regarding this demonstration, and will hold his company (now looking at my CEO) responsible for an explanation, tomorrow by 10 AM."

This followed by the congressman.

"Yes, Mr. Duncan (my CEO), we will be expecting a thorough examination and explanation of this. By tomorrow morning at 10 AM."

He promptly looked at me as he said, "Of course we will, and we will hold whomever is at fault responsible, I assure you."

And with that, everyone decided to head home. Except the ambassador, who was heading to a hotel since everything he and his family owned, was under three inches of water.

"Billy, I don't care how late you and Cam are on site here; find out and be in our offices at 8 AM with the answer of what went wrong. I have always liked you, but this thing is a disaster and we need to explain it and hope to survive it."

And off he went, as Cam and his technicians and I started to go floor by floor, finding one shattered monitor after another. And water everywhere.

"You know, Cam, I have always liked working with you; maybe we can work together again at my next job after they jettison me out faster than Petty's Hemi."

"Billy, I am so sorry; I don't know what happened. You saw the tests. Everything everywhere was green. I honestly don't know what happened."

And so, we searched, till 3 AM. And still found nothing.

"Billy, the labor laws of Washington DC will not allow me to keep the techs onsite anymore for today; I'll stay. Why don't you head home; if I find anything, I'll let you know."

"OK, if you can't find me, it's because I'm at a Red Lobster, filling out a waiter application. My cell phone's on all night. Ping me if you find anything. Maybe somebody will buy my Mustang so I can pay my bills after they fire my ass. Goodnight."

And off I went, home. At least there was no traffic, so I could fire up my Mustang and enjoy the ride. As soon as I got in, I turned on the news (which I had DVR'd) only to hear some ominous words.

"Tonight, the Norwegian embassy had a scare as it experienced a small electrical fire. Officials on site believe the fire was related to a new telecommunications network they were testing. There were no injuries reported, and the ambassador was quoted as saying their most valuable items, two priceless paintings, were saved."

Terrific. Two days, two debacles, and two newscasts. At least this one was local. If I had any luck at all, it would all be bad. And I drifted off to sleep on my couch.

Until my cell started going crazy at 5 AM. Then my house line which went to the answering machine. It was Cam calling.

"Billy, pick up the phone, please."

I did. "What in the world do you have? Nothing short of a time machine is going to save my ass."

"Wait until you see the video I'm going to e-mail you; it's from the main floor Telco closet, ten minutes before the speeches. It has to do with some people you'll recognize, and the power booster we had in reserve as a redundant power source for blackouts."

"Send it."

While I turned my laptop on, Cam said, "It's going to save us both. And cook somebody else. Two somebodies."

My laptop was finally on, and I clicked on the link, and what did I see? The ambassador and the reporter Connie Fitzgerald in a tiny telco closet… Making out! And leaning back into the CPU controlling the power! Which the monitor on it, is now fully lit, which means it was pouring additional power into the entire system!

"How on Earth couldn't they hear that thing turn on? It's loud as shit!"

Just then, we got an answer.

An aide to the ambassador burst open the telco closet door and said, "Ambassador, your wife is not twenty feet around the corner and looking for you. She wants a picture with you and the congressman before your speech! She is wondering where you are and mad as a hornet. Quick!"

And all three left. Quickly. But you know what didn't leave with them? The additional power being poured into the system, which, according to its monitor, was then glowing a full green, then five minutes later, amber, and then, ten minutes later, a full red. Then it blew up, sending sparks everywhere in that room, too, as they were going off in all sixty-four monitors. What they did was essentially double the electricity going to each device; it was only a matter of time till they blew up. All of which was captured on the video recording.

"Thank God the recorder is run off an independent battery system, or we would never have seen this.

"What in the world do we do with it?"

"I'm showing it to my CEO right after I tell him we have only one solution and it's not pretty."

"I have to admit, for an old guy, that ambassador has game; I mean that Connie Fitzgerald may as well be a super model."

"I know, but we have to figure out what gets us out of this mess. 10 AM is soon going to be here."

9:30 AM. Tom Duncan's office.

"That old dog, no wonder he wasn't screaming so loud. Maybe he knew he had something to do with it. I'm sure he has no idea we have this. I actually like him, so maybe there's a win-win out of this where he saves face and we come out as heroes. But that damn congressman has been on my ass since 7 AM this morning, saying investigation this, negligence that. He is one big pain in the ass, let me tell you. I almost wish he was on the tape. I'll have a call with the ambassador's IT officer, see if I can have a chat with the ambassador. Lay low."

Of course, I could lay low. That strategy saved me not two days ago. Now a Spielberg moment may do the same. And it did.

After our CEO privately spoke with the ambassador, he held a news conference in front of his embassy, flanked by my CEO and myself.

"We found out through the assistance of these gentlemen and their company, an older power circuit expired and caused this entire incident. Not only did their quick action save our building, this young man and his quick thinking saved two priceless paintings from damage.

We are forever in your debt, and I will recommend to our Premier you be made an honorary Norwegian."

Good God. I had to wonder if Madame Pearl was seeing any of this, and laughing or wondering "is that that young man who made fun of me?" My horoscope yesterday was certainly full of sparkles, as was my day. I couldn't wait until I read Wednesday's! I'd been so blown away the last twenty-four hours, I forgot to grab my paper. I made a note to myself to read it before leaving D.C.

The texts of support I was getting from several friends and family were priceless, too:

"Good God, you're on TV!! And not for being chased by cops!" (my brother, Tommy)

"How in the world did YOU save that thing?" (softball buddy, Scott)

"Are we allowed to borrow that embassy for a party now that you saved it?" (Mike)

"Your father wants you to get a haircut the next time you're on tv. Me, too." (Nice to hear from my mom, who just learned how to send texts)

"Did you ever get me Marissa's phone number? Can you please tell her I helped saved that Embassy, too?" (Mike again)

I must admit, this one was nuts; and, yes, I was convinced the debacle was tied to the horoscopes, but how could the Madame have known the ambassador would be making out with a news reporter in the closet?

My CEO was happy again, we were back in good graces with the United States Government, and I needed to get going to New York and coordinate with Cam the final touches of the Statue of Liberty project.

"Billy, I know this has been a bit of a hectic week, I want you to try and enjoy the New York trip; I know you're a huge Mets fan, and from there. If there's any chance you can catch a game, the company will pay. In the meantime, it's noon. You probably need to get in that race car of yours and get going."

And off I headed to the Greatest City in the World. New York City, home of America's Team, the New York Mets. And apparently still under some kind of voodoo spell with horoscopes. I could hardly wait.

***

WEDNESDAY
The Road Trip

Day five was here, and I was still reeling from the "sparks" and trying to come to terms with how all these accidents could keep happening. After the news conference where I was branded as a hero of sorts, I made my way back home to pack for my trip to New York. As I packed my car, I was also reliving my wild dog chase and the pool lagoon, and then Monday's worm fiasco. I could have been drowned or sued to kingdom come if my aunt hadn't stepped in to get that cake... As far as I could tell, there was no logical explanation for the chaos. Random chance was just not enough to cover the string of unfortunate incidents that I'd been plagued with—although, this latest one, while nearly giving me a heart attack and causing me to be a hair's width from being fired (and maybe even arrested), got turned around quite favorably. I was an honorary citizen of Norway!

Before I got on the road, however, I knew there was one point of business that *had* to get fixed or I couldn't go to NYC. We had a huge contract with the city of New York, almost top secret, which would utilize our technology on the statue of liberty. *The freakin' Statue of Liberty!* There was no way I could risk a worm or sparkle or a crazy dog mucking this up. So, my first order of business was to hit up Madame Pearl's for a quick chat, possibly some serious groveling—most likely some very serious groveling and make up for yesterday's talk. I was sure she'd see things my way.

I also needed to check my paper. I hadn't checked today's horoscope, but I was sure it wasn't "become an honorary European." So far, this curse had had no permanent damage, at least, nothing that I could see as of yet. But, after corralling Rusty into his cozy downstairs hideaway, I was running way late. I grabbed the paper and jumped in

78

the car after texting the two high schoolers who watch Rusty when I travel for work. Essentially, this is a mini vacation for Rusty, too, since he has the whole house to himself while I'm gone. The kids walk him each afternoon, and make sure he has enough food and water. A good gig for both.

I revved the gloriously powerful engine and took off, happy to be getting out of town and away from the office and everyone's scrutiny. Who knows if people were wondering about me. Had they connected my presence with the fiascos of the last two days? No clear signs either way. I pulled up my phone at a traffic light to check flights in case anything *really* bad happened tomorrow night at the Statue of Liberty. Never know. Maybe Wow Air had a cheapo flight from NYC to Oslo. I could hear it already:

"Why are you here, and what do you want?"

"As a new citizen of Norway, I'd like to move here, possibly get my dog brought here, and get a job in telecom."

"And why does it say 'seeking asylum' on your application?"

"Well, due to a rather large unfortunate event in which no one was hurt and that I was allegedly involved in."

"And what was this event?"

"The total destruction of a beloved American landmark, which was entirely not my fault, though many, many people, mistakenly believe it was. Did I mention no one was hurt? Because, no one was hurt."

"I see, wait right here."

Suddenly a horn honked loudly behind me; I'd stalled at a crossroads while the light had changed to green and I was still daydreaming about glaciers and fjords in Norway. I was at the stoplight which led, if I went straight, to the highway and back home to pleasant Virginia, or, if I went right, to my nemesis, Madame Pearl.

"C'mon you idiot!! Move your ass!"

Some guy was hanging out of his window and shaking his fist. Maybe that was today's curse: "Don't stop at the lights and daydream too long, or some rude jackass will hit you with a nasty song" Hah! That's a rhyme I came up with in three seconds—with a rude guy yelling at me. *Maybe if this telco stuff doesn't work out, I have a future writing evil poems for Madame Pearl for the next dummy she hits with a spell.* That was assuming, of course, I survived the week.

The Mustang roared to life and I quickly accelerated right toward Madame Pearl's. Maybe I should've gone straight and just forgotten all the chaos. Mike could have been right, still. Well, he'd been no help whatsoever. If he had been cursed like I was, he'd be thinking the same thing: get to Pearl's and get this fixed.

Regardless, it was 12:15, and I didn't have much time for groveling, I needed to get on the road quick, and be in New York by 8PM for a conference call with Cam and his NY team, and go over the Liberty project. Also, avoiding rush hour would be good. Rush hour seemed like a perfect place for Mrs. Pearl to flex her hex muscles. Or to risk a fight with another tough guy. Plenty of those types where I was headed.

On M Street, I couldn't help but notice that this city was constantly under construction, something remarkable considering it was a 250-year-old city. Cranes were everywhere, road crews, orange cones, all of it. And most of all? Traffic. I didn't know what these guys were always building, but I wished one of these years they'd build an entirely new layer of streets above the current ones so we could move faster around here. Maybe a mustang lane for people with cars that need to flex a little. Just saying. A move for the people if you will.

Well, just as I pulled up in front of Madame Pearl's, who did I see walking down the street? None other than Marissa from the Crazy Horse. I guessed she was on her way to work. She recognized me as I got out of my car.

"YOOOOU!" She pointed and nearly raged.

I didn't know how to react, so I shrugged and pointed back to myself: *who me?*

"My grandmother is mad at you; she wouldn't stop talking about it all the while we ate on Sunday. Every Sunday our family has a big dinner, and she wouldn't stop talking about how she was 'mad at that schmizaberg' and 'hopes he learns his lesson' and how 'he better stay away from my granddaughter' and on and on. She went on for like twenty minutes, until my mom got her to calm down. It's a good thing your friend left me such a big tip; that helped keep her anger at bay. Gosh, she's a mad woman when angry. I'd hate to see anyone go there with her."

Apparently, Marissa had not spoken to Madame Pearl yesterday, so she didn't know she was "freshly pissed" not just angry for the initial time we met. Who knows, maybe Madame Pearl had zapped me with another curse for my attempt to visit her and try to get a bit of a reprieve on this curse.

It was so nice to be recognized and among friends.

"That's great. I'm glad to see your grandmother remembered me. How is she? I was just in the neighborhood for work, and thought I'd drop in and say hello. Is she around?" I had to play it cool. What other move did I have? These people sounded scary as all heck and I needed a curse reversal, pronto.

The door to her House of Pain was locked. I knocked a few times while Marissa looked on with a cryptic smile.

"She's not there, and won't come in until three; she opens at four, or didn't you see the sign?"

I was all, "yes of course," and, "I beg your pardon," and if could only have a quick meeting, I could be on my way and out of everyone's hair.

Then I asked, "Can I leave a message with you? I'm late for a big event in NYC and...well...I just want to make sure no more sparks."

I laughed awkwardly. No wonder I was terrible at gambling. I had all the numbers in my head but couldn't keep a good poker face.

"Oh, so you want me to represent you, is that it? Hmm. Have you had anything unusual happen this week, per chance, since you think everything she does is fake?"

I thought to myself, not unless a dog nearly ruining a wedding, a swimming pool nearly drowning me, an e-mail that shut down thirty-five million cell phones, or an embassy that nearly went up in flames is unusual. I'm sure they were all coincidences.

"Ummm, no, everything's just fine. I've had a great week, and just wanted to say hi. She told me to stop by if I wanted, so I figured I would." I smiled weakly.

"Oooh. Ok. No problem."

She paused and looked me straight in the eyes with her arms crossed. I felt like she had magic powers, too, and was digging really deep into my soul. There were some good things in there, for sure, but some not so great things tucked away. I hope she'd see me for the good.

"By the way, didn't I see you on tv at some news conference with an ambassador talking about some kind of fire which nearly ruined rare paintings?" She took a step back and leaned into one leg.

"I was there, but that whole thing was way overblown. It was just some tv monitors that had an issue. It was no big deal. Anyway, I'm going to get going, I have to go to New York for work; I thought I'd drop in since I was here. Again, please tell her I said hi."

"Oh, sure I will. I bet a casual hello will make all the difference."

She was glaring now, and I just didn't have time for it. I started to wave and do my polite guy routine when she added, "Also, do you know if your friend Mike has a girlfriend? He came in for lunch and was so nice; he also left me another forty percent tip like he did on that other bill with all of your friends. I can tell the nice guys by if they're polite and leave good tips. He seems so different from other guys, and I think his volunteering at the animal shelter is just wonderful! Please tell him I said hi and to come back in!"

"Of course, I'd love it if you two got together."

Again, I was stunned at the lengths my friend would go to, the son of a gun. "Well, I have to get going, I need to be in New York by eight tonight."

Just then I got a text from Mike, speak of the damn devil.

"I got off work early and am in DC; let's grab something to eat at Marissa's restaurant before you head to NY."

I typed back quickly.

"OK, sounds good, I'm talking to her right now."

"Excellent; I'll be there in five minutes."

One thing about my friends and posse, they were consistent; horrible gamblers, not good at fixing things, and never to let an opportunity to meet girls go by. Mike was no exception.

"You know what, Marissa? Why don't I see if I can get Mike to come down and meet us for lunch? I think you guys make a great-looking couple, and I'll tell him what a great girl I think you are. He always listens to me when I have dating suggestions. Who knows, maybe we can sort out what's been going on this week, too! I have time for a quick lunch, then need to head to New York."

"You would do that for me? What a dear! I really like him, with all his volunteer work, him liking children, and puppies. He's just such a nice guy!"

"Not a problem, I just confirmed via a text he'll meet us."

And off we were to Crazy Horse for a late lunch, but then I needed to get moving to New York. I told myself I could earn back some points with Marissa, scarf down some grub, and skip out early, and with any luck get her in my corner to work on her Grandma.

"I can't sit with you guys, but I can be your waitress; and, Mike, it's nice to see you again. Your friend, however, I'm not so sure of. He made fun of my grandmother....*Again*...and she hasn't felt good this week, and, well, you know, you were there, he says everything she does is fake."

Marissa was leaning over and had her hand on the back of Mike's chair. Lucky son of a—it pays to say the right thing. That was a lesson I was surely going to learn.

I just leaned back and let them talk, sipping my water. Hydrate. Eat fast. Drive fast.

"I know, I've tried to tell him he should be more respectful of everyone, and, in fact, I think there might be something to those horoscopes and the spell. I even told Billy this after he told me what's happened to him the last few days."

I was stunned. Well, not really. At least the guy was consistent. I had too much going on to straighten that comment out or come up with a counter. I needed to get Marissa to tell me how to reverse whatever her grandmother did. I decided to hell with being right. I had to come clean.

"That's right, Marissa; the truth is, it's been a bit of a crazy week, and I'm wondering do you believe in this. You know the horoscopes, palm reading, and most of all, do you think your grandmother's spell may actually be possible?"

There, laid out for her to see. God or Pearl, please forgive me. Marissa, I delivered my buddy to you, the "nice guy" Mr. Mike. Please go easy.

She looked at me like she hadn't a clue what I was talking about, which was really mean and almost got me angry. Instead, I'd come prepared and pulled out of my pocket the four horoscopes and showed them to her.

Then I detailed the events of the last four days:

Saturday, running all over the place, the wedding cake destroyed, a reference to "a race, cake and eat it too, and ending with a challenge."

Then came Sunday's "don't worry, you'll just get wet". And, of course, I told her about the pool exploding.

And Monday's great Evel Knievel YouTube marathon, which was tied to an e-mail virus, aka "a worm," which, just coincidentally, I was told to look out for in my horoscope. I really enjoyed the coverage on CNN, too.

And to yesterday's "sparkles and lights" reference in my horoscope, and how I was at an event that lit up like the 4th of July. Indoors. At an expensive location, too, I added. And again, I really enjoyed being on tv in any way, shape, or form.

"Wait a minute! Let me see all of your horoscopes again."

She was playing it cool still. She was gonna make me sweat it out. *This family, I tell ya.* Not an ounce of mercy.

I put the clippings all out in front of her and Mike.

"I never noticed before any horoscopes rhyming. Every one of these is like a poem. None of the other ones in the paper rhyme."

Good God, she was right. All of the Leo horoscopes were rhyming; none of the other ones did. Mine were all like poems. And debacles matching the wording followed each day.

Just then Mike chimed in, "Dude, holy shit, I think this is true!" (*Mike, I could kick you sometimes*—but at least he was finally on my side).

Marissa looked at him and was sort of hurt. "I thought you always thought so anyway!"

"I do, I mean, I did. I mean, uhh I told him they were true. Now I'm really convinced."

I chimed in to help this idiot, because I got the feeling he really liked her. But, more importantly, I needed to get this curse reversed. Or fixed. Or whatever.

"Me too, dummy; that's why we're here. To get this stupid spell reversed. Marissa, how can we do this? Where's your grandmother?"

"She's home sick because she's had a bad flu the last few days, and she's not seeing anyone. My mom has been over there with her, and she can't work right now."

"Can we call her? Maybe see if she'll unzap me if I apologize? Does she need anything heavy lifted? I can do chores, too, if it helps."

"We can try. Give me five minutes. I need to take that table's order, then we can call her. Meet me over there by the video games. We can call from there on my cell phone."

So, Mike and I drank our cokes, while she took another order.

"I think she likes me; can I borrow your dog while you're in New York?"

"Dude, you can't be serious. I'm trying to fix this thing, and all you're worried about is a date?"

"There's no reason for both of us to suffer. And, hello! I'm here trying to help you. I came here, didn't I? I've listened to all this spell-junk, haven't I? Just let me borrow him for a day. I need to find a dog park downtown. Chicks like dudes with dogs. I'm borrowing yours and telling her it's mine. What's his name again? Who cares, I'll make one up. Rex sounds perfect."

"Ok, you can borrow him, but DO NOT let him get loose. I got enough trouble right now without getting a phone call about how he got loose and you're all sorry; DO NOT let him get loose."

This friend. What's a guy to do with friends like this? The thing is, he'd come through for you in a pinch, but really busted your balls, my God.

"Thanks, man. Alright let's go to the video games. She's over there."

At the video games, we overheard Marissa's side of the phone call.

"I think he wants to talk to grandma for just a minute; can't he for just a minute?" Marissa was talking to someone at her house. Just great. The old witch was asleep. Or maybe she turned into a bat and was flying around her house.

"Oh, she's asleep? Well, could you wake her up for just a minute? No. I'm not going out with him. This is not a boyfriend thing. He's not my type."

Then she turned her back to us and said, quieter, so I could barely here and I don't think Mike was listening, "I do like his friend, though. If he likes animals, and has a pet, like a dog, maybe I'll go out with him." Then louder, "There's no way for Grandma? Maybe try tomorrow? Ok, I'll tell them. Thanks, momma."

"Marissa, that was so nice of you to try for Billy; maybe I can come back here later tonight when I go to the dog park, and we can call again!" Mike was in advocacy role now that he had my dog in his back pocket. What a guy.

OK, story of my life: the only chance I had to try to fix this curse just went down the tubes, and this dummy wingman was now a lock with this girl. Who, by the way, was pretty attractive and if I hadn't been cursed, maybe I would have had a shot.

"You have a dog?"

"He's a boxer and just as sweet as pie. Still acts like a puppy."

At that point I'd had enough.

"OK, can we please hold off on the dog/puppy thing for now? Marissa, what's the deal with your grandma, is she ok? Do you think she may help?"

"My mom told me to call tomorrow. She's asleep right now and no way is she going to bother her. Maybe later today after she wakes up from her nap. No one dares wake up gramma from her naps. You think your curse is bad, just wait and see the hell to pay if she's disturbed!"

What a great family, I was thinking and was about to suggest I come back later when she turned to Mike and was sweet as can be, "Mike, what time can you come up here? Will you have the dog?"

"Yes, I'll be here around seven; and, of course, will have my dog with me. I do everything with him. Billy, we'll call then and will help. I promise."

"Ok, I need to get going; I have to be in New York tonight, and it's already late; I need to jet. Thanks very much guys. I really don't know what's going on, but, Marissa, if you could please let your grandma know I meant no harm, and if I offended her in any way, I am sorry. Thanks guys, I need to go, I hope you two have a great night. Uuuhh Mike, aren't you bringing your dog?"

Marissa looked at me and her eyebrows raised a bit when I said I didn't know what was going on, but quickly replaced that look with a smile when I mentioned Mike and his dog. *Jesus, I have lost any moral compass I ever had.* Pimping out my real dog to my best friend, another dog, just to save my ass.

As I turned to leave, I saw Marissa giving Mike a slip of paper, undoubtedly with her number. If it worked out, great. I needed all the positive mojo I could get. I just hoped grandma would send whatever good vibes my way that Mike earns with Marissa.

At that point, I needed to get in my Mustang before I got stuck in rush hour from DC to Baltimore.

When I finally got on the highway headed north, I knew this curse was definitely not over, but at least we had a plan. Mike and Marissa were gonna get together later that day or night and try to get her grandma in a good place to reverse whatever was going on. These horoscope predictions had been getting worse each time, and I was going to be working on the Statue of Liberty in twenty-four hours; I couldn't have it fall down. Especially if I was in it, near it, or seen anywhere around it. The crown alone on that thing probably cost more than my house, and my luck could only go so far.

Good God, I wished I were a writer instead of doing this telco stuff for a living. Those guys had the life; writing books, hobnobbing with movie stars if the thing was made into a movie. Actually, at that moment, I wished I was doing anything besides my current job.

Sometimes I wished I had never met Mike who, when I really thought about it, was the whole reason behind my woes. If he hadn't played along and made us go to the palm reading shop, none of this would have happened and maybe one of those ladies would have been more interested. At least I wouldn't have been plagued with near tragedy for a week and could have been spending time with my dog, instead of Mike. I swear, if that dog got Mike a girlfriend, he would owe me big time.

I was about to hook up a complicated telecom solution in maybe the most iconic landmark in the country, and at the same time, I was fighting spells and curses just for cracking a damn joke! A joke! Those two dummies had better come through for me; I needed a win.

My end destination was the Best Western of Queens, right near Citi Field, home of the Mets. I stayed at this place when I went to the 2015 World Series, Game 4, a gem pitched by Steven Matz until Daniel Murphy kicked a ball in the 9th inning and we lost, but the hotel was actually nice. And very well priced for a New York hotel; it was $135 for the night, complete with HBO and donuts for breakfast in the lobby.

Getting around the Washington DC Beltway was never fun, but midday actually wasn't bad; I scooted around at 60 mph, crossed over the American Legion Bridge, saw a really nice view of the Potomac River, and cruised for twenty minutes before I exited onto Route 95 North. The day was great for driving; sunny and bright, and the roads were dry. The temp? About 65, being April, it was still getting warm for spring, but this was just a gorgeous day, and I loved driving. I'd always done my best thinking when I'm in the car and rolling good.

I was thinking about if this spell was real or not, when "DAMN!" I realized I forgot to get a paper to check my stupid horoscope, and I was running late so I couldn't get one until I got away from the city. All the exits at that point in the drive were crowded. Along the way I was going to need gas, and then I would have a chance to grab a paper at some point after Baltimore. That's when it hit me. Was there a geographical restriction to the curse? Like, since I was outside of DC, did it not have jurisdiction or something? Or, Christ, what if other papers didn't have the same horoscope and I couldn't look mine up? After seeing how casual Marissa was, I had swung back to being skeptical of the reality of the curse. Also, I hoped it was just bad luck because I didn't want to be wrong. *Gosh.* I couldn't help myself.

Anyway, I was behind schedule and needed to haul ass. It was two and I was not even in Baltimore. I couldn't stop right now, anyway. I'd have to stop near Philly. Maybe a different paper would bring some good mojo; the Washington Post had done me no favors that week.

Baltimore came and went, and traffic was moving just great. If I had a horoscope, it couldn't be one involving traffic jams or bad weather or anything else, because I was jetting along at 70mph. Making good time. When I hit Philly, I'd even have enough time for a cheesesteak. The best there is.

With an eighth of a tank of gas in the Mustang, I reached Philly with a clear mind. No incidents and I had the guys in my back pocket. I was convinced Madame Pearl would forgive me and tomorrow would be career making. At this rate, I'd get a raise by the end of the month! I had to admit, being on the road was therapeutic. I had always been able to clear my head while driving, and I really needed it. I felt much better. But I was about to run out of gas.... One thing about this Mustang, it liked gas. A lot. I guess that's to be expected with a 429 Super Cobra Jet under the hood, with 400 horsepower. It's fast, it's fun, but it guzzled gas.

Perfect, there was an Exxon right off the exit. On a totally different and good note, since I'd been making great time, and a really cool thing about Philadelphia (other than the Mets routinely putting it on the Phillies) was they have two battleships that people could visit. On one side of the Delaware River, right next to Philly, is the battleship Olympia, which was one of those old white ones used during the late 1800s, that was a sister ship to the Maine (yes, the "Remember the Maine" that blew up—that one).

It was extremely cool, and not too overwhelming to visit. I'd actually been on it and it looked great. It was about three hundred feet long, mahogany wood all over the interior, beautiful white paint outside, and specifications that were tailored just for that boat. It was a good afternoon tourist site to work off your cheesesteak lunch. The other battleship on the opposite side of the Delaware, the USS New Jersey, which was technically in New Jersey, that one was enormous. Anyone who liked these types of things owed it to themselves to visit.

Both were museums and beyond cool, and you could get lost on the New Jersey because it was that big. Over three football fields long, and one of those giant grey ones used in World War 2, with the big guns.

I did love them as a kid. We'd drive down from New York in an old station wagon with the whole family and all of our crap and noise and hop out in Philly for a few hours on our way further south to the Beach. Since then, I had been on both a few more times as an adult and wished I wasn't pressed for time.

I pulled up to the free pump and selected premium. I was fantasizing about being on those ships and the cheesesteak I was about to pass on when I'd gotten in my car to get back on the road and nearly forgot to get the paper. Almost a disaster, but I was optimistic that this one was going to be a good one.

I parked the car, left it running, and grabbed a copy of the Philadelphia Enquirer inside the station. I flung out the unnecessary sections and flipped around until I found the Style section, which had the horoscopes. A quick check for Leo was:

LEO

*"Best to move quick and really slick
Like a well-timed Jiminy Cricket,
Or today may end, kind of rough
With a flurry and a really hot ticket!"*

What a relief! So easy! Don't go nuts and get caught speeding. Simple. The day had gone great, I'd actually made up time, and the Mustang was running like a champ. Being an optimist, I decided to believe in the power of positive thinking and was going to enjoy the rest of the day. I decided to take a quick ride over the bridge to Jersey, a flyby to see the battleship, then it was back to 95 North at 70 mph. You didn't get pulled for doing 70 on 95. Heck, you could usually do 75-80 with no problem, though 80 was pushing it, especially in a 'stang. You had to be careful when you had a cool car.

Getting over the Route 44 bridge was cake, and once on the other side, I just followed the signs to the battleship.

Man, the ships still looked great. I saw them from a distance while crossing the bridge, and driving around in the parking lot, you couldn't help but be amazed at the size of the New Jersey; it literally looked like an office building on its side, and the big guns (the three turrets) were just awe inspiring. Too bad they didn't fire these things off for the Fourth of July…I'd have given anything to see a misfire shell the stadium where the Phillies played (I still remembered them running up the score against the Mets, one time, 26-7. I think it was 1990, but I tried to block out that memory, particularly since I'd bet and lost money on that game).

I was about to get back on 95 and was cruising when I had a hankering for some music. Man, I didn't know how I could go that long without listening to something. That curse had my head all clouded. I checked the CD deck and I found a great Stones album "Exile on Main Street" set up and all I needed to do was hit play, which, I took my eye off the road for not even a split second, and when I reached over—it happened as if in slow motion—and *BAM!* I hit a nasty pothole! Hard. Thank God for my upgraded shocks and for going 50 miles an hour in the right lane while I was setting up my music. Mike gave me shit, but I always got to the slow lane when I had to mess around with anything on the dash for an extended moment. Had that been in the left, going 70, I might've taken off a wheel! It was a pretty loud bump, but the car seemed fine, so I kept on with the Stones blasting.

I was enjoying the tunes so much that I missed a turn off where 95 merges right and another local route veers from the left lane. It was no big deal. I had made good time and would just turn around at the next exit. I drove a dozen miles before a right-hand exit appeared, finally. *Sheesh.* I got off, made two lefts and followed the service road for what seemed like forever. After ten minutes I still hadn't seen a sign for 95, so I planned a stop at the next gas station to get directions. My cell phone, of course, had no signal out there in the middle of nowhere and I'd have to pull over anyway to engage it.

I decided not to stress. The day had been good, and I had plenty of time. Traffic was moving well, and the service road was scenic, at least, when, just at that moment, a car blew past me. One of those new Dodge Chargers, with a Hemi. Fast, bad, jet black, and it sounded like a race car. Being a car guy, and also in the direction I was going, I needed to speed up a bit to check out that car. I gave the 'stang a little push and pulled up closer to the Dodge just a mile down the road. It had the Hemi package, great steel wheels, and I couldn't see who was driving yet. And also, what did I see on the back bumper? A New York Mets bumper sticker! Not only was it a cool car, it's had a fan of my team driving it! Nothing like being around my people. I for sure had to catch up and see who was driving it.

I pumped the gas a little and expected a tatted-up guy with a beater and a sports cap, but it was a blonde, and it looked like—was she laughing so hard her head was tipping back? (I couldn't see too well because apparently, she knew how to drive a Hemi; fast). Again, a blonde Met fan, in a great car. How cool this day had turned out.

I nearly bought one of those cars back when I was shopping for one, so it was actually great to hear it roaring, which it did, and sped up ahead of me. I needed more time with it, so I pumped the gas. And I passed her easily, and, looking back in my rearview, I saw the driver was laughing again at God knows what. When I passed her, she did look at me for a second, and I think she waved to me! Maybe she liked Mustangs. Maybe she wanted to race? (I do not need that trouble, I stated out loud to myself.) Or, who knows, maybe she was just saying hi. There was a red light up ahead, so I planned on rolling down the window and asking her what was so funny. Why not, right? One thing about the road was, when you crossed paths with another driver whose car you respected, you always had a connection.

I got to the red light first, and she pulled up and lowered her window just as I did.

"Hi, I'm Billy, that's an extremely cool car."

"Thanks, I'm Annie. Your car is pretty nice, too, but I think something's leaking out of it; that's why I was waving back there. I was trying to get your attention."

Then the smell hit me; it was gasoline! When stopped completely, the fumes were unmistakable. Maybe when I hit that pothole, something broke. The bottom of the gas tank must have been hit and ruptured.

And at the same time as all of this, a jeep pulled up to me on my other side, and said, "Hey buddy, I have bad news, you look like you're leaking gas, and look way behind you."

And I did. And I saw it. Fire. Coming fast like a train following the trail of gas I left for the last two miles. Apparently, somebody had tossed a cigarette out of their car, and it hit the gas. Ignited, it was following the source. Which was me!

"JEESUS CHRIST! Look out!!!" I yelled, at everyone and no one and myself.

"Quick get out!" yelled the Hemi driver, who, if I had any time, I might have tried chatting up. Instead, I found myself praying and promising that if I survived this, I would come back to Jersey to find her.

At that moment, there was about 100 feet separating me, my car, and whatever gas was left, from flames, probable explosion, and God knows what else.

Both the Hemi and the Jeep saw this, and each turned off to get away from me. If either of them had any thoughts of being the cavalry, they quickly put them away.

Instead of jumping out, I floored it. The Mustang roared to life, and unfortunately, while it didn't have posi-traction (both rear wheels spinning), it could still haul ass and did, as it fishtailed for about sixty feet until the rubber gained traction and took off! And just in time; the flames were definitely gaining; I didn't know how fast fire could travel (I was about to find out!), but I was up to 75 mph and put about ten car lengths between us. I just needed to keep it that way until I figured something out.

I had no idea where I was and was just moving until I could find a solution that didn't involve abandoning my car! I could see the fire behind me, and the thoughtful drivers around me could too:

"Hey you idiot! Fire is following you! Pull that piece of garbage over!"

This from a guy in a dented-up pickup truck.

"Thanks!" I waved, while keeping an eye on the flames through the rear-view mirror.

I kept moving. What I needed was something to drive over and interrupt the gas. Thinking this over, maybe a better plan would have been to abandon ship. All I needed was my laptop bag; it had my project plans, the hotel info, all of it. Insurance would get me back most of the value of the car. Too late now. Cars were starting to slow up ahead. *Great. Traffic on a side road!*

There was no way I was stopping, and one good thing about this road was there was a shoulder on the right, and a median strip on the left. I wasn't stopping for anything unless it could put out fire. Then I had a great realization: maybe I'd run out of gas, it'll be exhausted, and no explosion! No luck, I have only lost 1/3rd of the tank; I'd need to drive around for an hour. *No way I'm gonna make it!*

People ahead of me had no idea what was going on until I flew past, only to be yelled at "Asshole!" Then they saw the flames about ten seconds later, then understood. I couldn't believe there wasn't a cop somewhere. I was driving like 65 mph in a 40 mph zone. *Somebody should be calling a cop by now!*

Great. I was speeding like a lunatic and I was coming up to a red light, with both lanes full. I knew I would be cooked if I stopped (literally) and had no intention to. It appeared if I stayed above 40 mph, the fire couldn't catch me, but I couldn't keep this up, as I zipped around an SUV who apparently thought I was number one. Or maybe he was number one. I didn't know and didn't care, all I saw was he had a single finger up while I zoomed past him. I had a red light to navigate! *Thank God for the shoulder.* And I drove right down it.

I had to admit, I was scared like crazy, but at the same time, impressed the high output engine I put in this thing was doing exactly what the mechanic told me it would. "When you drop the hammer hard, that thing's gonna fishtail your ass all over the place, but once it gets traction, it's gonna roll like the Concorde."

And so far, it had.

At the red-light (off the shoulder, I might add), after a few more helpful driving tips ("Jerk!"), I screeched around and made a hard right onto a long straightaway that was nothing short of heaven-sent. Again, the accelerator was down hard and I actually pulled way ahead of the flames (approximately 200 feet). Now I had bought myself some more time for a plan. Or an escape. Why weren't there any cops in New Jersey anymore? Where the hell were they? *All I need is one!* Maybe one who had a buddy at the Fire Department. I had a feeling those guys would be involved in this mess before it was over.

Well, I still had the straightaway, and I had just seen a sign that read "Keen Lake Campground 2 miles." A campground. With a lake! There was a God; *I just need to get two more miles out of this mess and get this thing into that lake!* As I drove, I reached back and grabbed my laptop bag. The way this day was going, I thought a quick exit was going to be needed, and I needed that bag. The entrance appeared and thank God no one was at the gate as I blew through it. (The flames were still coming but at least I'd managed to keep some distance between us). The park appeared empty, again, some good luck which I gladly accepted.

And then I saw it—the lake. A makeshift beach front with a bunch of plastic chairs and floatation toys. I wondered how deep it was; I wondered if I could get there, and, even if I made it, I wondered if this was going to involve a jail sentence. To steel myself I was repeating: *Fire is bad, and water is good. Fire is bad and water is good!*

I had slowed down a bit to make sure I knew where I was going, and the fire was gaining on me. It was back within 100 feet and, while

I didn't feel the temperature, I was feeling the heat! I needed to get this thing in the lake. I'd have to take my chances!

I came to the parking lot and made sure no one was around, then I zoomed over the curb, on to some grass, then passed through, and over, all the beach chairs, toys, and floaties. No wonder parents are yelling at their kids all the time to pick up their junk. *This is like driving through a damn yard sale.* The car actually started to get hung up on some things, and I immediately thought, *I'm gonna die and not even reach the damn drink,* until I saw it. A dock. *I'm going to find out just how much air I can get under the Mustang!*

It was not a second too soon. Apparently, riding over all that junk had widened the leak and way more gas was spilling out. I could tell by how the flames roared in the rearview, burning the stuff on the beach and raging like a giant wave of fire.

I punched the gas again when I saw two tables and powered through them, smashing them to bits, and hit the dock fast and was at the edge in a few seconds as the fire started chewing up the wood behind me and then... away we went! Just like Burt's Trans Am over that creek in Smokey & the Bandit. I believe I was about eight feet higher than the lake and sailed far. And yes, I had my seatbelt on, thankfully.

The landing was every bit as nuts as a you'd think a car hitting a lake at about 40 mph might be. It sailed out to about forty feet, splashed down hard, skipped and stopped. I was in about four feet of water. Ok, usually docks and lakes are deeper than four feet, but this one was man made, and the geniuses who made it, didn't want it too deep. Maybe it was a kids park thing (with the day I'd had so far, at least drowning was off the table). But I needed to get out. And did, with my laptop bag, cell phone and waded away from the car to a clear part of the shore. Since the lake was not too deep, I could go to a different edge without too much effort.

Gas was still pouring out, bubbling up from beneath the car and, one thing about gas and water is, yes, they don't mix, and gas floats. Which I didn't know at the time and so made a grave error.

Just as I reached the shore, the flames reached the trail on the water and found their way right to the car. And it did exactly what I thought it would do: bring New Jersey the Fourth of July in April! The one thing I could say about losing my car is that at least it went out how it came into this world and how it looked and drove: spectacularly!

A huge fireball blasted out of the rear window (this car *was* a fastback, so the explosion went up and out). If seeing my baby die a heinous violent death wasn't so painful to watch, it would've at least been a bit entertaining. Regardless, one thing I knew for sure was that car was not getting to New York tonight, and likely nowhere ever again. Except a junkyard.

I trudged across the shallows to the area where the beach front had been set up and righted a chair and sank into it. I watched the flames roll across the disturbed lake and begin to burn themselves out along the dock and the part of the shoreline I'd wrecked. I wasn't sure if anything could be worse. I wouldn't have felt this bad if I lost my buddy, Mike!

I sat in the chair, a bit dazed, until I heard police sirens wailing in the near distance. In a minute, two police cars pulled up. And in another moment one of the officers was at my side with his hand on my shoulder.

"Are you okay? Is there anyone else in the car? Do you know some girl in a black Dodge Charger? Boy is she pissed at you; something about you're a maniac."

And why not blow up my one shot with her while I'm at it!

After a few minutes of explaining and answering for the chaos I'd caused, the Fire Department (who I'd become more and more acquainted with these days) showed up and hosed down the area and the water. Funny, putting out a fire burning on the surface of water with more water. One of the firemen came over and said, "The fire's out, and we believe whatever gas was in that thing went up with it."

Thank God.

All I had was my laptop bag, and the paper, still turned to the horoscope:

LEO

"Best to move quick and really fast
Like a well-heeled Jiminy Cricket,
Or today may end, kind of rough
With a flurry and a really hot ticket!"

Well at least Jiminy Cricket didn't get a ticket. Or so I thought for a minute.

"Son, I hate to do this, but that car is an environmental hazard now being in that lake; I wish I could avoid it, but we have cameras on all of these vehicles, and we're audited daily, so I have to give you a ticket. At least we didn't see you speeding, and we believe that blonde has gone home; she was at the station for thirty minutes, mad as a hornet. Apparently when you peeled out, you kicked up a bunch of rocks on her car, and possibly knocked out one of her taillights. Just think of this as getting off easy. We would have had to cite you for reckless driving, speeding, running a red light, lane violations, driving in the shoulder, trespassing, breaking and entering. I'm sorry, son."

"Ok, I understand. Please give me the ticket. But back to that blonde. Did she say anything else about me? In the 3-5 seconds at the traffic light, I thought we had some kind of connection."

"Let me look. Yes, in my notes, there's something. Here it is. It would be a million years before I'd consider going out with that idiot. Yes, she used the word 'idiot;' Exploding cars is not a way to get dates, son. Let that be a lesson to you."

"Ok, so if I wait it out, there might be a chance?"

"I think this one's a long shot; maybe you should move on. I suggest you get your car out of the lake and consider that a win you weren't in it when it exploded."

Well, at least I was alive. The police were kind enough to send a wrecker they deal with out to the lake and he dragged it out with a cable that was unbelievably long. And despite the explosion, the car did not look that bad. The back-end glass and floor beneath it were gone, but the rest looked like it might be fixable.

"I'll give you three hundred bucks for it."

The tow guy was keen on taking it off my hands since he knew I was stranded.

"I'm gonna think about it; how about taking it to your station, and we talk in a few days. I need to get to New York tonight. Which reminds me, is there an Enterprise Rental around here?"

"Sure thing about the car. But keep me in mind, that car looks worse for the wear. Hop in and I'll drive you to get a rental. We'll get your car over to our shop asap, too. The owner's name is Ray, and he's a great mechanic, if anyone can fix that torched ride, he can.

We got to this Enterprise just as it was ready to close. I didn't say much on the way. The tow guy was eager to find out more about the story, but I didn't have the energy. I was bummed about Annie. Nice name, too. And then I was online and going over paperwork at the counter and the guy led me to the lot:

"That's the only car you have?" I asked the gentleman behind the counter, who also was apparently the owner

"Yep that's it. I wish we had more, but we've had a run on them. That sky-blue Volkswagen bug is all we have. My daughter used to own it and she sold it to me for the business. She loved it."

Not only did he run the place, apparently he stocked it with his own kids' cars. *Sissy cars too.*

My beautiful Mustang, gone up in flames (literally) and now to have to take this car, as girly a car as it gets.

"I'll take it. Thanks very much; I'll be back in a day or two with it." If that was all they had, that was all they had. Time to move on and focus.

I grabbed the keys, which were hot pink with a purple rabbit's foot attached and squeezed inside. I looked at my watch and it was 7:30. I was not going to be in New York to be on the call at 8:00, but I could take the call from the road, maybe, if I got lucky with service in my sky blue Volkswagen bug.

Somewhere Madame Pearl must have been smiling. At least I survived, and had five horoscopes out of the way, and only two left. I guessed I should feel lucky.

My new-to-me used bug had an AM/FM radio, no CD or iPod connectivity, and could hit 60 mph with the gas pedal floored over about twenty seconds. Not that I needed an iPod input anymore since it was on the floor of my once beautiful Mustang when it drowned and blew up. Maybe it could dry out, I was thinking as the city came into site on the horizon. Being a technical genius on all things electronic (as my posse would certainly verify, or, more likely, absolutely dispute, since I could barely program remote controls), I wondered if I could sit it in the sun and dry it out. Or wasn't there a trick with rice and a Zip-lock bag? Do they make car-sized Zip-Locks? If I ever saw it again.

Before I left, I told Ray I needed to bolt, and paid in advance to have him pull my car out, take it to his shop, and we'd talk in a day or so.

At a minimum, I needed a new gas tank, probably whatever connects it to the fuel lines, and a new back window. The back seats were torched, then half blasted out of the window. I gave Ford credit though, the frame did not look bent, nor was the back end warped (other than the taillights which were shattered). The explosion looked like it went straight up through the back seat and blasted out of the large back window on the fastback. Before said explosion, it looked kind of rough, like Mad Max's car; now after the explosion, it looks much closer to Max's car after that eponymous vehicle went up in flames, too. Who knew, maybe it could have been fixed. That engine alone was money. I considered patching it up and turning it into a rat rod (I had always secretly wanted a rat rod, and in fact had some dents on it already I had no intention of fixing). Ah, the bright side of things. I wasn't going to let Madame Pearl get to me. Even though this time she nearly got me killed.

I took my calls sitting in traffic in northern New Jersey, traffic I wouldn't have hit had I not taken that detour to Philly, had I left DC and not went to lunch with Mike and Marissa, had my damn car not blown up! The first call was very routine; I declined to mention my exploding car, or shenanigans in New Jersey, and just stuck to the project. It turned out, I needed to be at the Statue by 8 AM, which meant I had to be at the Staten Island Ferry by 7AM with the laptop to help line the telco dishes. All the guys were on the same page and we wrapped up quickly. I was determined that tomorrow would be perfect. No potholes, no racing, no seeing sites. All focus. The other guys agreed. We hung up as I hit the traffic for the George Washington Bridge and was excited to check out the skyline while crossing into upper Manhattan. Now I could make the calls I really needed to. To Mike, first, and find out what was going on.

Mike wasn't answering. I couldn't believe it. Straight to voice mail! So I called his house line and got the machine there, too.

"Mike, it's me, Billy, PICK UP!!"

I waited and sure enough, he picked up the line.

"Oh, sorry man, I thought you might be Marissa; she's not happy with me right now."

"What? Why? Did you guys have any luck with Madame Pearl?"

"Who?" I could have strangled him!

"The psychic who read our palms and cursed me! The whole reason we were at lunch with Marissa, who is the granddaughter!"

"Well, things were going great at first with Marissa. I went home, got your dog, and we went to DC to go to that dog park. It all started out great. I think she likes me. Or maybe did."

"OK, this sounds all interesting, but the mission was not a date; it was to get her grandma to stop being pissed, and reverse the spell; what happened?"

"Well, first it was all good; she loved the dog, and Dusty was being all cool."

"Dude, not that it matters, but his name is Rusty. Now, what happened?"

"Well, we were walking along, we got pina coladas at one of those outside places, and Busty, I mean Rusty, jumped onto a table of some couple, and knocked all their stuff all over them. I yelled at him, and he growled like shit, and she actually got a little pissed at me for that."

"OK, did you re-focus, and remember the mission?"

"I did; I said, let's all cool down, get another colada, and go to the dog park. Maybe we can call your grandmother about the spell, and, uh, Rusty may make some friends."

"Is my dog ok?" Now I was getting concerned. Yes, he was a pain in the ass, but he was my pain in the ass.

"Yes, he's one hundred percent good. Now, back to the story. We got another colada and made it to the dog park. When we got there, I let Rusty go and he was totally having a blast. Running all over the place, jumping on the benches, the tables, and even other dogs. It was like Disney World for dogs."

"Ok, sounds like what happens at dog parks worldwide. What about calling Madame Pearl?"

"I was just gonna get to that part, hold your horses. We were sitting there, talking about Rusty and all, and I noticed how pretty the sunset was and said 'Hey, check out that sunset, Marissa.'"

"She did, and she looked back at me and winked! Or so I thought was a wink, so I leaned in to kiss her, and she punched me! Hard, too. Man, it hurt. She can pack a punch. I've been slapped a few times by chicks, but she drilled me with a right cross like a boxer!"

I didn't give a damn. He deserved it. And when or if I got back, I might pop him too. I was happy she hit him! Except, that meant he blew his chances for me to fix my curse. Mike was really screwing me this past week. I had to restrain myself as I paid the bridge toll and took my place in line to cross the Hudson.

"*Okay*, and is there anything else?" I didn't want to know but had to ask.

"She told me she was not winking at me, but a gnat flew in her eye! And she really got pissed because when I tried kissing her, apparently it caused a contact to fall out, it was new and expensive, too.

Personally, I think those things are over-rated; I like glasses. Anyway, I thought she over-reacted, and told her so. Then she got even more pissed; some crap about her contacts were custom, I was a pig, and she didn't think I liked dogs, kids, or volunteered. I might have told her that the night we were all at her restaurant. Anyway, she was in no mood to call her grandmother and stormed off. How was the ride to NY?"

"I can't believe you did this! You sure my dog's ok and home?"

"Yes, I even fed him. He's all good."

Despite being furious, the view from the bridge was gorgeous and I could feel the energy of the city, and it took my mind off his totally effing up this small favor I needed him to do. I decided to forgive him, for now, and then briefed him about my ride, the exploding car, all of it. And how the horoscope in the Philly paper sounded very much like the train wreck of a day I had.

"Now what am I gonna do? I needed her to help make that call. Dude, how could you screw this up?" I couldn't let him off the hook entirely. I had to get my frustration off my chest. Meanwhile, midtown was lit up as the sun was already down and I could see the Empire State Building, three colors, and the Chrysler Building, my two favorite skyline buildings.

"I am so sorry, but she is smoking hot, and things were really going good; she dug the coladas, liked your idiot dog, and my mojo was working. If you need to blame somebody, I think Busty caused things to go south when he jumped all over the people at the café knocking all of their bullshit all over the place. It's his fault. You gotta put him down man, he's wild."

"Rusty. His name is Rusty; and don't try to pin this on a dumb dog. And no, I'm not putting him down dumbass, remember, Marissa's an animal lover. And besides, as the dog owner, only I get to blame him for things, it's a perk of the job. Ok, what's Marissa's number, maybe I can still catch her and see if she'll call, maybe get something positive out of this mess."

He gave me her number, and I hung up summarily without any goodbyes—that jackass—and quickly dialed her. I called several times and was on my fifth time as it hit 10pm and I was already cruising into Flushing, Queens.

Ringgggg… Rinngggg…. Rinnggggg…

"Hello?"

"Hi Marissa, it's me Billy; please don't hang up! I'm really sorry about whatever happened with you and Mike earlier. I just spoke to him and he told me. Can we please talk?"

"He is a pig! Tried to put the moves on me and made me lose my brand new contact at the park. And I don't think he owns that dog; he kept calling him Rex, and he had a thing on his collar that clearly said 'Rusty' on it. I told him so, too. All he kept doing was asking if I wanted another pina colada, then he made me lose my contact. I slapped him and he better not come back to my restaurant, or my brother's gonna beat him up."

I was really encouraged by all of this. And I shrewdly decided to let her tell me she "slapped" my idiot friend, when I knew she punched him in the eye. I hoped he grew a nasty shiner, which I would then tell all our friends was from a chick who *maybe* weighed one hundred and five pounds. There might be a God after all. *God I hope he gets a shiner.*

"I am so sorry, but I was hoping we could talk about your grandmother, and maybe if you had anytime to call her about reversing this spell. I really was hoping she would."

"Well, I didn't. I was so mad at your pig-friend, I posted what he did on Facebook, and all of my friends think I did the right thing, slapping him and all. I've been on an instant chat all night with them, and we all agree, he's a pig, and I was right. And now it's nearly 10 PM, and no way am I calling my grandmother tonight. She's been sick and going to bed early. If you're worried about the horoscopes, you're going to have to wait another day, and I may not even do it thanks to your pig friend."

"Would it help if I got him to apologize? Maybe in person at your restaurant?

"I'll think about it; I don't know if I like him anymore. He doesn't even know his dog's name, he's fresh, and rude, too. Call me tomorrow."

"OK. I completely understand. Thanks anyway. I'll give you a call tomorr--" The phone clicked as she hung up without another word.

The hits just kept coming. Maybe she'd feel like helping a bit more tomorrow. Oh, well. That was all I could do at this point. I pulled off the highway and within a few turns was at the hotel, hours later than I should have been. I didn't have time to eat or relax. I showered and got straight into bed, still smelling gasoline and burnt metal, and flakes of God knows what in my hair. Tomorrow would be a new day. For the first time in a while, I prayed for all the people I knew, including dumb ass Mike, and definitely Marissa, for her happiness and for grandma to get well. I didn't care anymore about the curse. I just wanted everyone to be good. I could get through it, or, at least I thought I could—I had to think. My last prayer was for Lady Liberty herself. Please God, I thought, let her be OK.

***

THURSDAY
Lady Liberty

I arrived at the Best Western in Queens, a place that I considered my home away from home while in New York. I called this place "Little Shea North." Why? Because I stayed at this same hotel when I saw the Mets in Game 4 of the 2015 World Series, the game where we unfortunately lost, when Daniel Murphy kicked a ball in the 8th inning, leading to a horrible Kansas City Royal rally that put us down 3-1 in the Series. Had we won that game, I was convinced Matt Harvey would have led us to victory in Game 5—as he nearly did anyway.

I was more than glad to stay in this hotel, despite the loss, and would stay there any chance I could get. I could have used the mojo of a friendly place after the chaos of my week: between dogs, internet debacles, thirty-five million cell phones going down, two stories on the news. Also, it had free HBO and fanatastico continental breakfast in the lobby—the instant coffee was overlookable, considering.

It was after 12:15, so even though it felt like Wednesday night, I knew it was now Thursday, so I was going to make sure I stayed in the room the rest of the night just in case anything, from a horoscope perspective, was in effect.

I didn't know if I could take another debacle right after surviving the lake and explosion, so I was just going to relax, watch a few minutes of tv, then get to sleep. I had to admit, despite my car going up in flames, it truly was a beast regarding its speed, handling, and just all-round bad ass performance. And I thought, from a driving perspective, Richard Petty would've been proud of me. Hauling ass around that hard right, then hitting the straightway (from Heaven, I might add again), driving on shoulders was kind of fun, and I bet the King (Petty's nickname among NASCAR fans) would've approved. And if anyone was wondering why The King had his nickname, all they would have needed to do was YouTube the end of the 1976 Daytona 500, and learn. Even in a loss, The King showed why he's the baddest man to ever drive a car; that blue and red Dodge Charger (nearly Met colors!) hugging the inside lane is a thing of beauty, and I am sure that car would've outrun the flames. Easily. I bet he would've figured out a way to outrace everything and keep the car from exploding. Despite coming up short that day in 1976, The King won more races and Daytona 500s than anybody ever will.

When I got tired my mind turned to my favorite moments in sports. It's just been a reflex; one I've become accustomed to late at night. It was 12:30, and I shouldn't have turned on the TV, but, out of habit, and pure mindlessness (I needed something else to think about) I flipped through the stations and settled on something boring and, I presumed, innocuous—WOR TV, the local news channel.

Unbeknownst to me, WOR TV covered a wider net of "action" around the tri-state area and, when I flicked it on, it was showing the "near tragedy" that took place in New Jersey—*my* near tragedy; yes, they had police dash cam film of my race with the flames. Apparently, there'd been a cop trying to catch up to me in part of my "flame-filled jaunt in New Jersey!"

The effect of seeing it from a different angle was pretty cool, I had to admit: my Mustang like a blur, the fire about eighty feet behind, and police and sirens blaring loud, all in pursuit. The program ended the feed before my jump into the lake, leaving their viewership in suspense as to whether the "perp" lived or died. Ha.

Despite being a lie, I had to admit it made for dramatic TV. Regardless, I needed to turn in so I could be on my A game for work on the Statue of Liberty. Which, I was extremely nervous about; I called the front desk, put in a wakeup call for 5:30 AM, and nodded off to sleep.

The next thing I heard was jostling.

"Look out Billy! It's coming down!"

And if I didn't see it myself, I wouldn't have believed it; the entire arm and torch of the Statue of Liberty broke off and crashed onto a tugboat, sinking it in a manner of seconds! Good God, I wondered how deep the Hudson was there, and how we were gonna get the torch back. And then get it re-attached; it looked like it broke at the elbow. I imagined the girls giving me a hard time about the Met pitchers--this thing was going to need the biggest Tommy John surgery ever. "Paging Dr. Andrews, Dr. John Andrews: please bring your scalpel, and a ton of cement. And a bunch of green paint." This was bad—really, really bad.

"Cam, keep your eyes on the sinking location. Maybe we can use the crane and some rope!" I chimed in, not really believing in that as a possibility.

I was in the Crown about to look again at my Red Lobster applications when all of a sudden all I could hear was this loud ringing. What in the world could be installed in this stupid statue that could ring that loud! Damn! As soon as we find that arm, put it on, and spray paint it green, I'd find that bell and turn it off!

Just then, I rolled over (still in my bed, in Little Shea North, aka the Best Western), and realized the bell that was ringing super loud was the phone next to me, and it was my wake-up call. Thanks to the guy at the front desk for being prompt. It was just a dream. Granted a horrible one, but still just a dream.

I immediately thanked God, reminded anyone up there watching that all my previously offered deals (no smoking, cursing, gambling) were still on the table, behaviors I would no longer participate in if the Statue of Liberty remained unscathed by the end of the day.

If by chance, the arm, crown, her head, any part of it fell into the Hudson, I would have been forever grateful if I was way, way south, (did I mention way South?) if such a thing were to happen. And if it did, of course, I hoped no one was injured other than Lady Liberty.

This was how I started my day. At least the wakeup call got me out of that horrible dream. It would be a shame if my first visit to Lady Liberty were to go down like that. When I lived in New York as a kid, my family took in all the cool sights, seeing the Empire State Building, the Bronx Zoo, Little Italy, but we never visited the Statue of Liberty, and now I was going to be inside it for the first time ever, for probably the next eight hours! Carrying with me a terrible curse...

Hopefully, if all went well, I would be on the way home to Virginia tonight around 5 PM. With any luck, I could return the rental if the Mustang was drivable. I just needed no more excitement and started to wonder if a quick call to Madame Pearl, combined with some very convincing groveling coupled with profuse apologizing, could somehow make this day go smoothly. I was about to call her when I got a text in all caps from Mike.

"BILLY, PLEASE CALL ME NOW! I NEED TO TALK!"

Wonderful. What in the world now I thought as I quickly dialed him.

"Billy, thank God you called. You're not going to believe this. I called Madame Pearl like we talked about, and she was pissed at me, something about dis-respecting her granddaughter, which I totally don't understand what the big deal is, then she said to be careful, and mind my own business when I mentioned you were sorry."

He was stammering and was pretty worked up.

"Ok, so she said to mind your own business, do you think she'll take my call? Did she sound like she was, you know, nice like a Grandma?"

"I don't know, man, she asked me if I was the one with the dog, and the kiss and slap, and I said maybe I was, or maybe I wasn't, but that matter has no bearing on why I'm calling. I also asked if Marissa was a forgiving type person, and she promptly said that perhaps I should mind my manners, or I, too, might get stung! Then she hung up on me!"

"Stung? What does that mean?" I asked.

"I think she meant she was gonna zap me, too, with that horoscope thing she got you with. This morning when I went to get my paper, three bees were by it, and they went after me. I was half asleep, and then I remembered what she said to me… So I opened my paper and read my horoscope.

"Listen to what it says, dude. I'm so screwed, because I'm a Scorpio, too:

SCORPIO
"You're pretty quick to step into affairs,
That are not your concern, nor should you care,
So do yourself a favor and stay out of these things,
Or learn how to run or endure some mighty stings."

"I got stung getting the paper! She's pissed at me too! And when I took out the trash a cloud of gnats chased me. Christ…. you were right…. *I got it, too!*" Mike was clearly all in on the horoscopes now.

"Oh, so now you believe this stuff? It's all real now that you got a couple of bugs messing with you? Jesus Christ, I've been on tv, my car exploded, and I allegedly was involved with an email virus that possibly affected a few million cell phones. Poor baby. If you didn't screw things up by hitting on Marissa, maybe Madame Pearl would've chilled and we'd both be out of this mess. I hope a lightning bolt lights up your ass tomorrow for trying to get lucky and jamming us both up. Dumbass."

I couldn't help but enjoy Mike's turn of fate. He probably deserved it.

"Well, what are we gonna do?" Mike was suddenly all about the solution.

"If I were you, I'd get some Raid bug spray and lay low. And I hope you have a big-ass shiner from Marissa. I'll try to call Marissa or Madame Pearl today if I have time. Now, I have to go. You may remember, I have to install a bunch of tech-crap on the Statue of Liberty today, and there's a pissed off psychic who drilled me with horoscopes that aren't flies. I hope the damn thing is still standing when we're done. Who's the pansy now? You almost got stung by a bee, I nearly died a couple of times!"

We agreed to chat later that day or the next and he said he'd lay low and keep to himself.

"No talking to chicks, grandmas, or even pets! I'm staying in my basement in the dark."

Well, that was exciting. That dummy had been making fun of me all week, and now he was upset because he'd been stung by a bee. Good. *Maybe the next time I need help he'll be less of a hound, and more of a pal.*

Anyway, I had to get up, check out, and get my ass to Battery Park by 9:00 AM, so I needed to move quick. The only way to Liberty Island, was by ferry from either Ellis Island near the Jersey border west of Manhattan, or from Battery Park at the southern tip of Manhattan. (And the boat trip was at most half a mile by ferry, not long at all). Cam and his crack team (the same crack team as the Embassy installers) would be there. I wondered how much fun those guys had the other day. I decided they (even Cam) were on a "need to know" basis about Madam Pearl and alleged horoscope curses, so I had told them nothing. That was the wise path to take; besides, I doubted they'd believe me anyway.

I packed and headed down to the lobby for the most welcoming donuts and bagels in the tri-state area. Also, to my surprise, a much-improved hot cup of coffee. Since the install should be completed around 5PM, I was going to drive home that night, so I needed to check out of the hotel, and take all my junk with me. If the Mustang was ready, I'd swing by and pick it up, if not, I'd have to hang onto the VW for the ride home. Both the mechanic and the car rental place had told me no later than 7PM, so it would be a tight schedule, but I could keep the VW for a few days if I need to. *Oh joy!*

I was traveling lightly these days since my luggage got torched. All I had was my laptop bag and cell phone. If all went well, I'd be on the way home after we completed the install and testing. We had a low frequency antenna we were going to install in the torch of the statue, which would significantly reduce dropped calls in lower Manhattan. Our company would benefit greatly from improved efficiency and from calls routing through our tech. We were going to significantly improve the cell phone network for lower Manhattan as well as surrounding areas of Brooklyn and Jersey.

The device we were installing would route phone traffic more efficiently in the short term and was scalable as needed in the long term. A great fit for the city and speaking of fitting, the tech needed to be in the Statue's torch for the best focal point. What made this particularly important for my company, was no one else was being permitted to install any equipment on the statue. Our company had obtained an easement and won the contract, and because of us we would help all licensed carriers to boost their signals. This installation would alleviate the bad history of low capacity in the financial district for all carriers, *and,* most importantly to me, would make our company the focal point of the success of it. It would undoubtedly lead to more business with all of the major carriers, and definitely be a huge career boost for me. It was also my idea! This was my baby and I was going to be on point.

On the other hand, if things went badly, it would damage our reputation. If the statue itself was damaged, we'd be famous for all the wrong reasons. And I'd hate to think about what would happen to my career…

I grabbed my food and coffee and took up a spot in the lounge since I had a few minutes to kill before I needed to leave. Besides, the baseball highlights were on the TV and there was always a minute to catch up on what the Mets did last night. The bagel was amazing— again, I wished we had these in DC—and the coffee was much better than before. I tried to not let my happiness dull my edge. I needed to be on the look-out for catastrophe, so I meticulously reviewed my route to avoid slowdowns and roadwork. If I left the hotel at 7:00 AM, I could take the Cross Island Expressway, in the sissy VW, and link up with the BQE on the other side of the Pulaski bridge and avoid a 30 minute slow-down. Then I had the option, depending on traffic, of crossing one of three bridges or even using the Brooklyn battery tunnel to get to Battery Park by 8:00, and easily at Liberty Island on time. Cam and his team already had a crane transported to the Island via barge, and it was already lined up for installing the antenna. As a precaution, the city had closed off the monument until we completed our work, which would take the rest of the day.

I finished my bagel and put a lid on the coffee to bring it with me and as I made my way past the breakfast spread, what did I see? A copy of today's paper, the NY Daily News. The Daily News was my personal favorite paper because I worked a delivery route for the company as a kid when my family lived on Long Island. Under normal circumstances, I'd be a bit nostalgic about this and I likely wouldn't be able to resist checking out the great sports page, but, right then, I was concerned about the horoscope section, which I found on page 47. I held my breath, said a quick prayer and then:

LEO

"Despite your good efforts
To always work when you tire,
It may not be enough
to prevent her from a fall and a fire!"

Oh my God! A fall and a fire? That jackass had called me about bee stings, and I was going to be working on the Statue of Liberty, who may fall or catch on fire? Holy Shit!

Ok, I was concerned, but how could the Statue of Liberty fall? It must have been something else. There was no way the Statue of Liberty was ripping loose of its pedestal and taking a fall. It could have caught fire. I suppose that one actually had me more concerned.

I tossed the paper back on the table and grabbed an extra donut in case I hit some unforeseen traffic, in case I needed to eat my nerves away. How in the world could that thing fall off the pedestal? Maybe an earthquake would do it, but we were on the East Coast; I didn't even know if earthquakes even happened on the East Coast. No way. We were probably in the clear with the statue, or the horoscope was simply not related to it. Either way, if I didn't get moving, the only thing that would be falling or on fire, was my job, my life, and if things really went south my freedom. I chugged the rest of my coffee and headed out to my car.

As I scanned the parking lot looking for my mustang, my eyes settled on a powder blue VW Bug and I was about to question who in their right mind would be driving a car like that when I felt a dull pain in my gut as if I had just been punched. At night I failed to notice the host of bumper stickers, consisting of flowers and birds. Wonderful; would it have killed the guy to peel off his daughter's stickers before using the car for renting? From "saving the owls" to "don't use plastic" to "kittens are people too," this car was covered in stickers. There was a batch of daisies in the corner saying, "please don't step on me."

If I wasn't late, I thought I might have taken the time to peel them off, but this was New York, and I needed to get across the Island pronto.

In I went, and a quick look at my GPS told me the trip was only 14.2 miles, but with NY traffic it was going to take 45 minutes. No problem, it was 7:10, I had good directions, a car that's not on fire, and I was as motivated as ever to get this job done. And safely, at that. All I needed to do was keep an American monument from falling down somehow, and I was golden—until the next damned horoscope.

I was ragging on the VW, but it actually drove really well in the New York traffic, which, thankfully, wasn't terrible. The VW could corner and cut into lanes and was pretty zippy. It didn't have the same power as my car, not even close, may it rest in peace or, hopefully, rise from its sodden ashes.

The weather was gorgeous. A spring day which gave me hope that this curse had run its course. Looking ahead on my GPS, I knew I'd stay on the Long Island Express way for about 8 miles, then head onto the Brooklyn Queens Expressway for 4 more miles, then I had several options but I was planning on going over the Brooklyn Bridge (built beautifully of stone way back when), and then it would be literally three turns until I reach Battery Park.

I was going through everything one more time—Cam and his team would already be there with the crane—when, *wait a minute*, with a crane! That thing could do some damage. That was it. *The danger is from the crane*, I thought. *I better get my ass over there and make sure* that *doesn't do anything wrong*. It may not have been capable of knocking Lady Liberty over, but a crane could knock her arm off like I had dreamed about. I needed to warn Cam, but I couldn't tell him about a curse.

I dialed Cam's number and it went to voicemail, so I left a message.

"Hi Cam. Billy here. Just wanted to check in. I'm on the way. Have you and your team done inspections and is everything in tip top shape? Remember the embassy? We can't have anything go wrong. I know you guys are great but even the smallest detail we can't overlook. I know it sounds paranoid, but I have reason to believe...well, I just don't want any accidents. Call me with an update."

Regardless of Cam and his team, I had to get on site as fast as possible.

Of course, that's when I encountered traffic on the BQE, a raised highway that traverses the edge of Queens and Brooklyn. We inched across the Pulaski Bridge and the rate picked up a bit. I was anxious and worried about the crane, but the brownstones and row houses had me reminiscing. My grandparents lived on East 26th Street behind Bedford Avenue for over 40 years, which was just a few blocks off the highway. It was always nice visiting them and I wished I had more time to cruise the neighborhood. Their house was made of brick, a row house (like essentially most of Brooklyn), and was as solid as a fort. I mean that place felt like it was made of concrete; just a solid, three floor townhome, and an alley in the back.

When we were kids, my parents would take us there, and to small local restaurants and corner bakeries (all mom and pop places) which were just great. My grandparents had long since passed away, but it would be really cool to see parts of the old neighborhood. Next time I was up I'd schedule a free day to visit. Long Island (where I lived growing up), was full of smaller houses which were nice, and had yards. The closer to New York City (like Queens, and especially Brooklyn), space gets tighter, and you saw more apartment buildings, and row houses with less green patches. But the energy was amazing and hard to resist, though I liked my quiet, green neighborhood in Virginia and couldn't ever leave it.

The traffic picked up and I could see the Brooklyn Bridge come into view, stately and now sort of out of place amongst the supremely tall metallic buildings. What a treat to drive over it though, with pedestrians biking and running, tourists snapping photos even this early in the morning. And, in a flash, I was at Battery Park where, thank goodness, they'd cordoned off six spaces for us in the public lot three blocks down, where we could easily catch the ferry.

As I pulled into the spots marked "Liberty work crew" I heard, "Hey girlie, can you please keep your bug off to the side? I need three spaces for my truck; I need to wheel this equipment with my crew onto the ferry and need a straight space."

"Sure," I said, rolling down the window with a huge grin while watching the guy's face turn from annoyance to surprise.

"Sorry, bud. I couldn't see you too well; and with all the stickers and stuff, I thought that was a girl's car. Is it your sister's or something?"

"No, it's a rental; mine is broken down, and I have to be here today. We're installing the telco gear on the Statue." (I immediately reminded myself to call Ray in Jersey to see what the prognosis of my car was; maybe from the ferry I'd call him.)

"Oh, that's right. My name is Paul, and we're with NYC Parks. We have to test the props and tents for the upcoming Spring parade. Since you guys are on site and they closed the park for the day, the city is combining projects to minimize the days the park needs to be closed."

"Cool. I'll move the car."

And it was no big deal, we had six spaces, this guy had a large van with a trailer apparently full of equipment. I was glad I wasn't involved with that work, but he had three guys with him to help with transporting the gear.

"We have a ton of stuff so we're going to catch the 9 AM ferry. We'll need the extra thirty minutes, and we'll see you over there."

"Sounds good, I'm Billy, nice to meet you guys. I'm going to catch the 8:30 ferry. See youz later."

It had been so long since I'd heard "youz", and it brought me back to those younger days that I'd recalled on the ride over. I'd forgotten how much I missed it the tones and accents of the city.

The ferry was not too crowded and off we went, the river slapping against the bow and a salty breeze at our backs. Just so you know, it was 18 bucks for a round trip, but it was New York where things are more expensive and, while I don't like throwing down a twenty for slow ferry rides, I'll get reimbursed via an expense report. Cam and the technicians had already gone over on a private barge with their equipment. Since I was just bringing myself, I could arrive later on the public ferry. And now I wondered if I could put my car on that same report. I doubted it, but I thought it could be worth a shot, and if it wasn't accepted I'd tell the guys in accounting it was a joke to test their focus and to get back at them for winning a bet we'd made for the Super Bowl—lucky sons of guns. Anyway, I was on time, had a great seat on the deck, and planned on enjoying the ride after I gave my mechanic a call and after I checked in with Cam again.

A quick dial got me to him:

"Cam! Mornin' pal. I'm on the ferry on the way over. I should be there in about twenty minutes. How do things look, and how're the boys?" He and I work really well together, and that embassy mission just made us even closer. We both considered that a career ending project until he found that security recording. Maybe we should put a bunch of those cameras up today, just in case.

"All looks great Billy, me and the boys got over this morning at 6 via the tugboat that brought the barge with the crane on board. It's deployed on site, and we're anchoring it down now with the steel chords, and also the leveling bevels. We should be ready to hoist the antenna receiver around 11 AM to the torch, and then work the install. Two weeks ago, we ran the co-ax cabling up the superstructure inside it, so today all we need to do is install the dish and machinery, turn it up, run the signal tests, and we're out of here. I bet by 5PM we're one hundred percent done. How was your ride up?"

"I had some car trouble, but nothing too bad, though I had to get a rental."

I decided I'd tell him about all of it later. We had a lot to do, and I didn't want to jinx us by talking about some wacky things which may or may not have been from a curse a local palm reader zapped me with. I still needed to get through today and tomorrow; *no need for me to start complicating things now.*

"That's too bad. Well we're set and will wait till you get here before we go any further. And don't you worry. I got your message and we are taking all necessary and even unnecessary precaution to make sure no accidents—trust me, I remember the embassy. Maybe we should set up some of those security cameras just in case there's some hanky panky behind the scenes, Hah!"

He was on point as I expected, and I was laughing at the reference.

"Sounds good, pal. I thought the same thing, let me tell you. And I know you can handle all the details."

We hung up as the boat approached the midpoint of the harbor. I could see Manhattan behind me, Brooklyn and Staten Island to the left and Jersey on the right. It was a great site that I wanted to sit quietly and enjoy, but I gave my man Ray the mechanic a call to see if the hottest car in the world had any hope.

"Hi Ray, this is Billy, the guy who owns the Mustang. Have you had a chance to look at it yet?"

"Yes, in fact. Structurally it's not too bad. You, of course, need a new gas tank, fittings, a new back window; from an interior perspective, the rust under the back seat actually helped. The blast went up and through everything easier due to it being weaker and left the drivetrain alone. I think if I put a new tank on it, and trouble shoot the electric stuff, you may be able to drive it. The engine did not get flooded with water due its high-performance gaskets, so there's a good chance it's not damaged. I can get a tank in it today; the glass and seats will take longer."

"That sounds great. If you can get a tank on it today, and get it running where you think it's safe, I can come get it, and get the rest of the stuff when I get home. How's that for a plan, want to try that?"

"Sure, give me a call around 1PM, I should have a much better idea. I think this is very do-able. By the way, one of my guys wanted me to ask you if he could buy it. Says it looks just like some movie guy's car that blew up, and he wants to leave it like this. Mad Marty or something. I have no idea what he's referring to. Any interest in that?"

"Tell him thanks, but I'm gonna pass. I really like that car and if it can be driven, I'm gonna drive it home."

"Ok, hit me up at 1. Let's see where we are then."

"Thanks, Ray. Talk later."

And just then we pulled up to Liberty Island, and I had to admit, the Statue of Liberty was absolutely gorgeous on a sunny day. I did a smidge of intel gathering on it, and found out a few things. First, It was twenty-two stories tall overall; five for the pedestal and seventeen. for the statue. When we first got it from France as a gift (thank you, again, France), it was the tallest structure in New York City. Too cool. France gave it to us as a gift in 1876 (part of the Centennial, but it took ten years to actually design, build, and ship it to the U.S. 1886 was when it made it to NY! The reason it was green? It was made of copper, and over the years oxidation on it had turned it green. Originally it was the color of pennies! Again way cool. And the thickness? The sides were not thick at all. The statue was literally a skeleton frame, covered by copper the thickness of two pennies, and inside a spiral staircase made by a French engineer named Gustave Eiffel, (the same Eiffel who built the Eiffel Tower). I was still stunned that it's covering was only two pennies thick!

Anyway, as soon as I hopped off the ferry, I snapped a pic of the pretty Lady Liberty with the sun pouring over her crown. It felt good to be here and I was happy for this job. The statue was a historic gem, and best of all, I could crawl all over it today. I just hoped we don't have some debacle that knocks it down, or an arm off, or her crown off. I didn't think Madame Pearl was that cruel or powerful such as to have a bunch of birds pick the statue up and cause it to "sail away." What if it was not birds, but those spooky flying monkeys from the Wizard of Oz? It would take a zillion birds but maybe only a few troupes of those guys to carry this thing off; and if they did show up, there'd be nothing I could do because I was terrified of those creatures back in the day. Actually, I'd rather have that then some knuckleheaded telco installers break something.

"Glad you made it, Billy. Let's go over this, then get down to business. This statue is extremely cool. And, believe it or not, these guys have a great snack stand over there, so we're good for lunch, too," Cam said.

I loved New York; bagels and hot dogs on every corner, and even at the monuments. If only I didn't have this horoscope thing hanging over my head, I might actually have gotten to enjoy this. If I survived this week, and Lady Liberty, too, I'd definitely be coming back for some Met games to see them with 40,000 other great Met fans in Citi Field. Maybe by then I'd have a date to bring.

A quick tour of the statue confirmed what I thought; the base or pedestal had five stories in it, and you entered it and went up via an elevator. The statue itself was much slimmer and, for that, you needed to take the spiral staircase for 17 stories to get to the torch and 12 to get to the crown.

But the view from the base faced New York City and was just gorgeous. To the left, about a quarter mile, was Ellis Island. Yes, with all the history, and coolness. I would have to go there. My grandfather came over from Scotland with his family in 1923; I think there were some names from our family listed over there. I needed to find out, but I definitely would be back. A straight-ahead view was Manhattan, and the new World Trade Center, surrounded by the amazing NY skyline. Again, way cool. And behind us, about another mile, was Staten Island, where my cousins lived (everyone else had moved to either Jersey or Florida). It really was nice to see these places again, especially on a great day like today.

After touring the statue to get a sense of the scope, we went back down to coordinate with the guys at the base of the crane and to check connections on the ground with the network. Then, we were headed back inside to the gazillion stairs which actually numbered three hundred thirty-four steps from the heel to the crown, and forty-two more to get to the torch, where we are going to put our repeater dish. The repeater weighed about six hundred pounds and was the size of a refrigerator. Once this thing hoisted up via crane, two of Cam's technicians would install it.

I'd be coordinating all activities from a support perspective, from the torch, and essentially be backup if needed for anything. So, the tour was over for me until we were done, though, again, it was very cool. It was time for me to be at my station where I could see the whole process of installation. The guys were all in position and I needed to give the go ahead.

Cam was coordinating all activities from the crown, as well, and his lead tech Joey and I went up to the torch. Two more techs, Tim and Hank were on the ground level, and would monitor the crane. They needed to get that half-fridge up there (around the torch was a platform that could easily accommodate this), bolt it to the platform, tie in the power and cabling, and then turn it on.

This would be easy; the trick was getting the crane to maneuver around the torch, without bumping into anything. I had to admit, I would pay *the city and my bosses* for this opportunity! I was literally at the top of the Statue of Liberty with an unbelievable view of New York City! *Too cool!* I dispensed with the sightseeing and narrowed my brow to the task. Cam was calling me on the two-way radio; we needed to get going.

"Billy, you guys ready? We're going to get started. Tim and Hank are down working the cranes. We're all set and going to get this going shortly."

"Joey and I are all set, and in position."

Cam and his team were moving the dish up between two cranes, which would suspend it between them. The reason we had two is redundancy, in case a cable or crane failed, and at least having one would keep the unit from falling. At the end of the day, this thing would be over twenty-three stories high, and we had to lower it carefully onto the platform around the torch. I got a front row seat to maybe the coolest install I've ever been part of. But I had to stay vigilant and couldn't become just a casual spectator. The sailing thing was weighing heavily on me, but no birds and, at least not yet, no flying monkey-things.

"Ok everyone, let's start; remember we're in no rush, take it slow."

The two cranes were about fifteen feet to the right of the base of the statue, and essentially would raise the telco cabinet at a rate of five minutes per story. All in all, it should have taken just about an hour and forty minutes to reach me at the top of the head, and about fifteen minutes more to get to the torch. Once there, both cranes would pivot towards the torch, and lower it onto the platform around it. Once they lowered it securely to the platform, Joey would bolt it to the platform, and hook both the power and the coax cable to it. We could then begin testing it to make sure it was fully online and functioning.

It was around 11 AM, the crane had the gear fully loaded and was ready to begin raising it, and it was at the base of the statue. By this time, the Parks and Recs team had arrived, and were setting up their equipment, too, well beyond the perimeter of the statue. They were probably about one hundred-fifty feet south of us, behind the statue, each of us in our own sphere. I couldn't see what they were doing from my vantage point, but Tim met them in the parking lot, and they told him they were going to test some floats for an upcoming parade the city was going to hold in a few weeks.

Tim relayed this information to Cam since he was in the crown and needed to know where everyone was. Joey and I could chill for a few minutes in the greatest vantage point in the city, the torch. Just then the cranes began to raise up the cabinet.

So up went the two cranes with, suspended between them, a telco cabinet that was the size of a refrigerator and weighed about six hundred pounds. It was all going well—slowly, but well. While I was waiting, I figured I'd give Marissa a quick call to see if she cooled off from our conversation the other day, and hoped she was up for calling grandma and making sure my day went ok. She may have been angry still from our last conversation, but I wanted to try. How mad could she be? Besides, I was agreeing with her for punching that dummy, I don't know why she hung up on me. Anyway, I needed to call her and see where she was in all this, and if a call to her grandmother was gonna happen. Hopefully I could get a call in with granny before the team was finished. Also, I wanted to give my mechanic a quick call for a status on my car. Everything was under control and that crane was moving slow as all heck to be maximally careful.

The Marissa call went straight to voicemail. Being the optimist I am, I figured she was busy, and not avoiding me. I left her as charming a message as I could muster, regaling her with some of the details of my view and wished her and her family all the best, and hoped to hear back from her while the Statue was still in one piece.

Then I called Ray my mechanic, and had better luck.

"Hi Ray, it's me, Billy. The Mustang guy."

"Hi kid. Things look pretty good. You got lucky. We have a gas tank we just installed, and it's running great; no leaks. We have to replace some bulbs in the taillights, but after that, she'll be able to drive you home. I have a line on a back window and may be able to get you a back seat, but for that stuff, it'll take a few days. If you want, you can probably drive it home tonight. It still looks rough, the paint is torched in the back, but it's structurally sound."

"Outstanding!"

I was thrilled and told him I'd give him a buzz after five and get the payment set up then. Finally, some good luck! Yes, my car might look rougher than it did, but at least I could drive it home. I could always scoot back to Jersey to pick up the parts if I didn't find them back home. When that thing went up in flames, I thought it was done. Who knew that a rusty floor, and a back window would actually save it? Too cool. Anyway, even though I was just watching, I needed to pay attention incase these guys actually needed me.

"Billy, come in. It's Cam."

"Hey Cam, what's up?"

"Do you know what these guys behind the statue are doing? And why?"

"Yeah, they work for the NY City Parks and Recs Department and are testing some floats for a parade in a few weeks. Is everything ok?"

"Those guys are inflating a bunch of superheroes for like a Macy's Parade or something, I guess. Batman, Superman, Spiderman, looks like the shark from Jaws, and I think Wonder Woman, too. Looks pretty cool, but they're all over the park back there."

"Are they in the way?"

"No, they're far back; they're ok. Alright, keep your eyes open. We're getting up towards the crown."

And true to his word, the box came up and was approaching the torch. The best way to describe it was two large poles, pointed slightly toward each other, with about twenty feet between them. Between them, of course, was the refrigerator sized box, being held by cables connected to each crane. It looked very solid but also precarious at the same time.

"Almost there. We should be good to go…" and then there was a very loud BANG! Did I say loud? Well it was loud as shit! I was looking right at the cranes, and the equipment and nothing moved, so it wasn't that, but it was so loud I ducked in confusion and surprise. Being twenty stories up, surrounded by cranes precarious floating boxes tended to make one a bit jumpy. Especially with the week I had just been through. I wanted to recheck the horoscope in my bag, but I wasn't taking my eyes off the cranes. Which, thank God, looked just fine.

"Cam, did you hear that? What was that?"

"Bill, we're ok, and so are the cranes, but you're not gonna believe this; something just happened to those big ass balloons, and they are starting to float. All those jackass superheroes are not attached to their cords. They're floating free! It looks like the Jaws Shark busted, which is probably what we heard, and three guys down there are running around them trying to grab ropes to tie the balloons. And no, they are not being successful; Batman just started floating towards the dock, and Superman's moving, too."

"Ok, so Jaws is gone, and a couple of them are floating; are we ok?"

"I think so, but Spiderman just got loose and is floating towards us. I don't think those idiots can catch him."

Just then, a strong gust of wind sealed it: Spidey was loose. Cam was narrating the scene as people down below were running around and frantically grasping at the rope and calling for backup.

"Bill, that damn Spiderman is headed right for us. We're going to lock the cranes in case it hits us or them. Stay tuned."

What the hell else was I gonna do? Well, the thought of hauling ass down twenty-two flights of stairs did cross my mind, but how much could a floating balloon do? I was about to ask if they had a gun or a projectile to shoot down the balloon when they came in over the radio.

"Hang on boys, that damn thing's headed right between the cranes!"

And then the amazing you know whose giant head hit a direct bullseye on the suspended box, which knocked one of the locks off the attached cable, detaching it from one of the cranes. All in all, we did have two, so it's not like it was sailing to the ground, but what it was doing was swinging loose, like a pendulum. And right into the side of Lady Liberty.

And since the Statue was hollow, and made of copper, guess what a six-hundred-pound refrigerator sounded like? An enormous gong!

"GOOOOOONNNNG!!!!"

Great! This damn thing *was* going to get knocked off the pedestal! Just then, another GONG! The crash had my ears ringing and I was a bit stunned, not knowing what to do. That stupid thing (unbeknownst to me because I couldn't see it and was *not* going near the railing on the edge in case it hit there, apparently was swinging in a giant circle, like a yo-yo, around the statue).

GONG!!!!

The only good thing about this situation was the box was swinging lower than the torch (I actually think it might've knocked the arm clean off if the pendulum hit it) and was hitting the side around the shoulders.

"Cam, quick, come in; how are you guys, and what the hell is happening?"

"Bill…hang tight, the crane below is pulling back a bit, so hopefully it'll stop hitting. Hold on!"

"GONNNNNNG!!!!"

Would it have killed Cam to have wrapped that thing in some more padding? Even crappy movers wrapped stuff in blankets! I thought this project was at the Statue of Liberty! I felt like I was stuck inside a gigantic Liberty Bell.

"GONNNNNNG!!!!"

"Helloooo… Anyone. Come in. I thought you said it was going down! Jesus, Cam, that thing sounded like it was right under us!!"

"That's the last one, Bill. And look, count your blessings; Joey It's a good thing I'm fifteen stories away from those dummies and their stupid balloons, all of which are loose by the way."

And just then, I figured it was safe enough to get a peek out the window and what did I see? Batman headed north, up over Ellis Island, floating toward the city. Superman? Well, apparently, the Man of Steel had had enough of this party; he was floating South towards Staten Island. If only my cousins still lived there, I'd give them a call, maybe give them a head's up to see him flying overhead. First, I would have played a little trick on them and bet them some cash that they'd see Superman today. They, like I do, loved to bet. I think I owed them a few hundred, come to think of it. Too bad, I could have won my money back. I'd be sure to call them if the balloon turned toward Jersey. And just when I thought the show was over, who decided to float past? None other than Wonder Woman.

Now, under normal circumstances, I wouldn't mind seeing Wonder-Woman up close, but not today. Not when I'd had one mess after another happen. I was thinking of the horoscope now but these balloons didn't seem to be fulfilling the prophecy. Maybe this was just a true accident. What did that stupid thing say again?

LEO
"Despite your good efforts
To always work when you tire,
It may not be enough
to prevent her from a fall and a fire!"

Oh no!! This stupid statue might still fall. Forgive me Lady Liberty; you may be the only element in this with any brains at all.

And just then, Wonder Woman's foot got caught on Lady Liberty's pointy crown, and her head hit right into the torch. A direct hit, shaking the torch and the arm with a giant thud. Thank God the copper arm was acting like it was made out of steel, or it would've busted right off. And being in the torch with Joey, I had no desire to go flying down fifteen stories. We may not have fallen, but what I didn't see was the natural gas torch we had with us got knocked over and torn from its hoses. Which immediately started leaking gas out in a menacing hissing sound. Which Joey noticed right away. Since it was next to him and the railing.

"Billy, we gotta get out of here! That thing's gonna blow!" shouted Joey.

"What? Cam look out, we're coming down," is all I could muster as we both ran to the hatch at the top of the torch and jumped down the stairs, hearing another loud noise as it blew. God only knew what's going on in that torch, but at least the arm was still on as we ran down to the shoulder.

And it was a good thing we didn't see it, because, if we had, it would've probably given me heart failure. What happened was the soldering torch was torn away from the gas hose and ignited, sending a huge flame shooting straight up into the NY sky, about twelve feet high. And this was not a one-time flame either, it was being fed by the gas lines we tapped into, which meant it wasn't going to stop until the gas was shut off. Not that I could see it as I ran down the arm, followed closely by Joey, but at least it was shooting straight up! Lady Liberty falling was no longer a concern of mine. I was thinking explosions, fire, and again, the destruction of a national icon. *Great, just think of all the TV coverage this will get!*

We quickly reached Cam in the crown, and he was surprised to see us.

"Are you guys okay? I heard a large boom, what the hell's going on up there?" he blurted out.

"We're fine, but there's another problem, the soldering torch broke loose and blew up something up there! I think it's still burning!!" Joey stammered.

And just to make sure our blood pressure stayed up, then Wonder Woman was caught in a gust of wind and blown right back into the crown, hitting it hard, knocking us off our feet. What we didn't see was her leg and foot also hit the points on the Statue's crown and put two giant holes in her leg which acted like a jet, causing her to take off like she was sporting a jet pack. And she started flying in super-fast circles, until she ran out of air. Or helium. Regardless, she was out and crashed right down into New York Harbor. Or better put, she *fell* into the harbor!

As I helplessly watched this from the crown, I secretly wished I was flying with her. There was a fire upstairs in the torch, I had no idea where the telco cabinet was, and I was quite sure I would need a good attorney before the day was over.

Just then Cam took the situation by the horns. "Are you guys ok?"

We both nodded yes. A worn and stunned yes, but still an affirmative.

"All right, we have to do something about those flames." He quickly called his tech below, Tim and Hank.

"Tim, or Hank, come in right away!"

Tim immediately piped in: "Cam! Are you guys okay up there? Hank and I saw flames flying out of the torch!! And Wonder Woman popped and sailed over us real fast!" Tim added

"I know! I could give a rat's ass about the balloons, we need to shut the gas lines off, quick, go to the 1st floor control room in the pedestal. That's where the gas junction is where we tied our lines to. Get your ass in there and shut it down! *Now!* Call me back when you do!!" Cam shouted

What seemed like two hours was really two minutes, when we heard from Tim:

"It's all shut off, the gas gauge feeding the lines is showing zero pounds pressure! It should be one hundred percent off!" Tim said

"Thank God," was all I could get out, which was followed by a quick, "I could use a drink."

"Me too, Billy," said Cam, "but we need to see what's going on in that torch before we celebrate. Joey, go check up there."

Joey had had enough of this project. "Why me? The last time I was up there, the place was shaking, shit was on fire, and those balloons were all over the place. I didn't sign up for this shit! You guys go."

"Alright, stay here. Billy and I will go," Cam said.

As we gingerly climbed the stairs back up to the torch, I thought to myself that never before had the words "Give me your weary" meant so much to me as they did today. Thankfully, when we reached the torch, the flames were indeed out. And thankfully the only thing that was burned was a backpack holding some tools. The entire high-wire BBQ was over in less than five heart stopping minutes.

"Well, Billy, we got off easy," Cam said as he reattached the torch to the gas lines. "I have never had a week like this. First that Embassy fire, and now this. Boy I can't wait until the weekend. Let's head downstairs and regroup with everyone, then see about finishing the install. I see some police down at the base, we'll probably need to explain some things. Let me do the talking."

Anyway, at least we were out of danger, and, yes, there would definitely be some fall out over this. But it wouldn't be directed at us, or me for once.

We all met in the base of the statue, some of the techs looked a bit shaken up and happy to be back in a safe place. I felt better, too. My knees had stopped shaking and, while my ears were still ringing a bit, I could hear everyone ok.

"It looks like the Statue has a couple of dings on the back. If you dummies were going to hit a part of it, you picked the right part."

This from the Port Authority officer. He made no mention of the fire—apparently, he had not seen it. None of us saw any reason to enlighten him. And if things went south, we could always remind everyone the balloons caused it all.

Then Paul, leader of the overinflating balloon team chimed in.

"Is there any chance we can keep this between us? I mean no one was hurt, and Batman's stuck on a telephone pole on Ellis Island, and I heard Superman's hung up on some trees in Staten Island; all we need to do is fish out Wonder Woman, patch her and Jaws up, and we're good to go. I think we should keep this among friends."

Just then the NYC Harbor Patrol showed up, towing the giant Amazon lady. "Any of you boys looking for a giant date? Please take her back!"

Then Cam spoke up, and reminded me why I have always liked him:

"Guys, if our telco gear works, and there is no damage to the Statue that needs any official reporting, I say we put this little incident behind us, and we all go on our merry way. We have no problem doing any of that, just as long as we have no liability. My guys are good, and we can do this installation now. And those balloon guys tried to catch them; in fact, one of their guys took about a 50-yard ride with Spiderman before letting go."

And that's exactly what we did—which further showed why New York is still my favorite city: the people. They stick together. I secretly told myself they were all probably Met fans. And the Port Authority Police gave the balloon guys maybe the biggest present of their lives, definitely their jobs. And if anything got on the news, they could always say no one got hurt, and all balloons had been apprehended. And Lady Liberty was still standing, (thank God!).

So, after Cam verified the telco gear was not damaged, he and his team completed the ascent with a reinforced cable and hauled it to the torch. Once it was up there, the install was back on track, and they easily finished it. I was extremely relieved when I heard Cam tell me on my walkie talkie, "Billy, all the systems are showing green, nothing looks out of sort. If you want to take off and head home, we'll handle it from here."

Wonderful! The installation was complete, the only thing damaged was Wonder Woman, and I left her repair in the capable hands of the

NY Parks Department who freed the entire batch of Superheroes. I hope they were better at patching balloons than hanging onto them!! Thank God this was over, it was time to leave before something else happened.

I had never been bored in the Big Apple, and my record still stood. Off to Jersey to get my ride!

***

STILL THURSDAY

It was exactly 6:05 PM when the ferry got me back to Battery Park, and the VW was right where I left it in the front row of the "Telco Workers" reserved spot. All looked good, except when I walked up to it, I saw on the windshield a folded piece of paper. It was a flyer of some kind.

"Join us this Saturday, in Brooklyn, for the Flowers of New York Expo!" on it was a hand-written note: "PS – my daughter has the same cute colored VW. Please join us! Hope to see you Saturday!"

I couldn't help but notice, there were no flyers on the balloon guys' trucks, nor the banged-up pickup from the NYC Parks and Recs manager. Maybe they had run out. Regardless, I wasn't sticking around for any flower festival. I was out of there. I needed to be in Jersey by 8PM to get my Mustang (*or what was left of it*), or I'd be spending the night in Jersey. I really needed to get home tonight if at all possible; I'd been away for too long without professional care for Rusty. The kid next door to me had been visiting my house to keep Rusty company and to let him out in the back yard. To keep the dog from destroying things in the house. In short, I needed to get home asap, which means it was time to fire up the flower-mobile and get rolling.

While driving, I decided to reassess the entire week and the damage, possibly clear my mind.

A mental scoreboard of the week looked a bit like this: There had been six horoscopes, the dog/wedding cake incident, the pool, the embassy, the flaming car, the Statue of Liberty project, resulting in some lasting damage—one car, one rep, fear galore, anxiety galore, several fires, and some downed balloons.

Yes, I had been getting a week-long beating, and the only good thing about this week was it was almost over. I only had one more day of this torture; at least I could see an end in sight.

I decided I could try to enjoy the ride to Jersey, but then my cell phone beeped. While in the Statue, I, like many people in lower Manhattan, didn't have good cell coverage. Looking at my phone, I could see it said I had four missed calls, and four new voicemail messages. I decided to check them.

Message one:

"Billy, it's Mike. I finally got Marissa to cool off, and I think she may call her grandma. I told her I was really sorry about the other day, and I think her grandma zapped me with a spell with bees, and if she could help me out of it. I told her I race part time and would love it if she came to one of my races. She accepted, and said she'd call her grandma but now I need to borrow your car as proof I race. She even told me she didn't mean to punch me that hard. Call me buddy, I think I fixed it for both of us."

Message 2:

"Hi Billy, it's me, Tommy, the dog walker. I don't know how to tell you this, but Rusty dug a huge hole under the fence in the backyard, and wouldn't answer when I called today, and well, he's loose!! I am getting my dad and we'll try to catch him! I'm so tired from chasing him! We don't know where he is!"

Message 3:

"Hi Billy, it's Ray. About your Mustang, I was wrong, it needs another shock on the right rear wheel. If I let you take it as is, you'll lose control and swerve off the road and have a bad fall on the first curve you hit. I need another two days. I'm really sorry. Call me."

Message 4:

"Hello? Billy? It's me Rhonda from work. The President of the company just tried calling you to let you know there is a problem with the signal at the Statue of Liberty, and for you to call him. He said this issue may cause him to miss his kid's sailing competition and he is super pissed. Also, he heard that some balloons got loose in Manhattan and wants to know if you knew anything." Rhonda was our company President's assistant. Fantastic.

Wait a minute, many of the words in the messages sounded familiar:

"Despite all your efforts"

"Tired?"

"You *may have a fall?*"

"A *fire!*"

I had to check again and make sure, so I pulled over the VW at a truck stop and pulled out my horoscope:

LEO

"Despite your good efforts
To always work when you tire,
It may not be enough
to prevent her from a fall and a fire!"

Holy shit! Each message was using words from this latest horrible horoscope! All the other days, it was just one disaster, this thing was now hitting me like a tsunami of psychic shit! Four new things, all bad, and I was still not even home. *What the F is next?* "Fall, a fire, tired? Despite efforts blah blah," this curse was now acting in multiples! It was getting worse! It was a damn horror-scope!

I almost said to myself, "At least the you know what didn't fall down today," but I didn't dare utter those words out loud. My life was such a jinx-filled disaster, I decided to not tempt the Gods any more than they had been and risk jinxing everything now. When I left, Lady Liberty was standing and in one piece. Maybe the torch was a bit singed, but that was it.

I had to call Madame Pearl, see if I could get some reprieve. I tried her number three times and kept getting voicemail.

I then tried Marissa and got her voicemail as well.

Then I decided to try Mike and see if he could call Marissa, and my phone died due to zero battery. And of course, my charging wire was in my Mustang. I was radio silent until I got home.

I then floored the VW and got to the warp speed of seventy for the rest of the trip home. I was not returning this ride tonight, since I had no other way to get home, and I needed to check on my, apparently missing, dog.

Thankfully the rest of the ride home was drama free, and I pulled in front of my house just after midnight and shut off the car and headed inside. Hopefully my dog walker and his dad were able to capture Rusty. I could use a little luck. Yes, he was a pain, but any dog person knew these pets really were your best friend, and I needed one right then.

128

I gingerly opened the front door to my house, and who greeted me by nearly knocking me over? An eighty pound, four-legged freight train.

"Rusty! I thought you were gone!! Thank Goodness. There is still a God."

I got the front door closed and found this note on the kitchen table:

> *Me and my dad caught Rusty down the street. He ate up Mrs. Preston's flowers. She was pretty mad, but I distracted him while my dad tackled him. He was good almost all of the other times, he just ate a picture off the wall; also, he took a box of the Girl Scout Cookies. Oh, lastly, he ate a book. Me and my dad plugged the hole by the fence with a piece of wood.*

Thank God. And Mrs. Preston I'm sure would let me know how much I owed her. At least he's back.

Ok, I thought to myself, what picture? A quick look yielded the answer. Apparently Rusty was not a fan of Darryl Strawberry. He tore off my wall a two-foot by three-foot framed picture of the great Mets slugger and chewed through the cheesy frame. Rusty was following me around while I took stock of his handiwork, almost to say, "Where are you going with my new toy? And do we have any more?"

I decided to take him for a quick walk, even though it was super late. One thing about dog walks was they always helped clear my mind. Despite the occasional crazy tug from Rusty every time he sees a squirrel or deer.

While walking, I had a couple of things to think over; a torched car that would cost some cash to fix back up, another day of a potential horoscope gone bad, and how it started. I did not mean to insult anyone over this horoscope/astrology stuff. I really thought it was kind of hokey, *but* this week was giving me some second thoughts. What if any of it was actually true? And did it matter if I believed it or not? I didn't think so. But maybe I should have been a bit more open to what everyone else believed about this goofy stuff. Who the heck knew if it was real or not? No one.

What I really thought I should do was do fly-by to Madame Pearl's and see if bygones could be bygones. I really did not mean to insult her. I resolved to use my day off to swing by and apologize to her, regardless of what it meant to the last horoscope.

And I wasn't going to ask her to reverse anything if there was anything to even reverse. It was not that big a deal; I believed (and was holding my breath while thinking this), I would very likely be employed regardless of what may appear in tomorrow's horoscope. My car? It had already been torched and could always be replaced. My house? If it went up, I had insurance; I just needed to make sure that dummy dog was out. So…that left my health, which, thus far, had not been at risk in any of these debacles. Regardless, though, I would apologize to her. And not ask for anything in return.

After a good walk, and some quality time with Rusty, I felt relieved. Though there were still some other big problems. I might lose my job, Mike had tied any help from Marissa to a car that was wrecked and still in New Jersey, and the President of my company was looking for me. And let's not forget, this party had one more day of a horoscope. With any luck, I'd be driving by the White House or some expensive stores in Georgetown when the next curse would strike me down with a fire or a worm or god knows what!

***

FRIDAY
There's No Place Like Home

If ever the phrase "Thank God It's Friday" applied to a week, and to somebody, this one was it and I was that person. I'd had several elements, fire, water, electricity, animals, and e-mails (are the last two even elements?) conspire against me in one form or another, and let's just say I was ready for the weekend. Just being home and sleeping in my own bed was therapeutic. My house may have been messy from time to time, and not the fanciest, but just like Dorothy said, "There's no place like home." By hook, or horoscope crook, the week was nearly over, I saw the finish line, and I was home. One more day was all I needed to get through.

As much as I needed to rest, I had responsibilities to address; first thing was call work and see what was going on with the Statue project. After that, I would deal with Madame Pearl and any apology. Then there was my poor, blown out car. While I loved it, it was way down the list. I sat at the table with a pad and pencil to take notes on the call and then draft an apology letter when I remembered one final *big* thing.

Let's not forget one more horoscope to deal with at some point, too.

I quickly called Cam to see what was going on.

"Cam, it's Billy, the President of my company is on my ass over NYC. What's going on? I want to know before I call him. Is everything still OK?"

I tried to tone down my panic, but I was having a hard time given how much of my ass was on the line—all of it.

131

"We've been on the phone all morning with the NY Park Police and we think we're good. There was a little bit of a mess from some of the torn balloons, but it's all under control now. We may need to spray paint some of the statue to cover a few burn marks, but we can do it and it'll look good. You probably should come back up when we do a final walk through in a day or so."

"Great. I guess that's why the president of my company was all pissed and calling me. Tell me, have you seen anything on TV?"

"No, the only TV people here were asking us if we saw any of those superhero balloons flying everywhere. We said no. Between you and me, we made a deal with the balloon guys. If we didn't see their balloons, they didn't see our flames. I think it will be all good."

Cam was a real quid pro quo, handle all the BS kinda guy, which is why I liked working with him. He'd never let a friend go down in, uh, well, flames.

"Thank God," I said with an exhale. "OK, I'll be back up there as soon as I talk to my guys here."

We were good with the plan and we hung up so I could reach out to work before the day started.

"Hi Rhonda, it's me, Billy, can I talk to Tom? I think he had a question about the Statue of Liberty project."

"Yes, Billy, he's been anxious to speak to you." Rhonda was trying to be polite, but I could hear the urgency in her voice. Clearly Tom had been angry, and I worried she'd gotten the brunt of it.

"Billy? Is that you? What the hell's going on up there! I've been getting my ass chewed out by some asshole in the NYC Mayor's office all morning. Oh, and late yesterday, too!!" Tom Duncan didn't hold back. I was about to tell him we had the wires solved and I'd be going back shortly.

"Not only did I have him on my ass, some jackass in Public Works got all the way up it, too. Double whammy! Do you know what that feels like to have two of those city knuckleheads on your ass? Not fun. Not one damn bit. Did Lightwalkers do this installation?"

He was furious and I wasn't about to tell him that I'd not felt that "double whammy," as he put it.

"Yes…well, no, but…" is all I could get out before he hammered me again.

"Well, tell those idiots to pick their damn tools up, and also their ropes."

"Ropes, sir?" I stammered, not having the slightest idea what he was talking about. All I knew was it wasn't the statue's torch really being on fire. Something about tools or rope left on the job site, and somebody bitching.

"Yes, dammit!! Ropes and tools, and something that looked like a giant flag. What the hell did you guys do, throw a Fourth of July party up there? I better not hear any damn reports of beer cans. I already told the mayor your ass is on the way back up there today, and you will walk the entire site, and there will not be one single scrap of trash, coke can, or a single M&M on those grounds. Is that clear? I nearly missed my kid's graduation over this. Now get in that hotrod and move your ass back there quick. Keep me posted."

Clearly he hadn't heard about the fire, my car exploding, or anything else supernatural, and far be it from me to ruin the man's morning with any more "whammies." I'd get the VW moving as fast as it could go back to NYC right after my pit stop in DC to see Madame Pearl, though I wasn't pleased with this turn of events, having to drive north again. At least I could see the Madame and I knew she opened at 4PM, but Marissa told me that on Fridays she goes down there early to do her bookkeeping, and other chores, so there was a good chance she'd be there. I was really hoping to have a nice chat with her, tell her I was sorry for insulting her, and make sure to not blame her for anything, and if there was one last horoscope I had to endure, so be it.

One thing that was a bit concerning to me was that throughout the week each debacle got progressively worse; early in the week I was simply chasing a dog. Now, I was trying to deal with the repercussions of setting fire to the Statue of Liberty! Calling this a full week would have been an understatement. I didn't know what day seven had in store for me, so I was dreading reading the paper. But, one thing positive about me, if anything, was that I was brave.

I powered through things that would cause many people to crumble. I was actually doing well for all the torment and pressure I'd suffered. And I was particularly brave when I had my posse, or my work dudes like Cam, or even my eighty pound dog (which I did now, at my side chewing on an old slipper as I patted his musky, loyal head, though I trusted him only as far as I could throw my torched Mustang), so I was going to get my paper, and read it, and deal with the consequences, again. Alone. Regardless of what was in there. But I would tip-toe going to get the paper. Just in case.

The Washington Post, April 29th, 2017. I couldn't care less about the front page at this point, though I did flip to the Sports (the Mets won—of course I looked). Then I paged through the rest. Metro (check). Food Section (check, didn't care anyway). Weekend (it had book reviews, which I'd actually started to read for some reason), but, holy smokes, no Style Section! Where were the horoscopes?

"Are you kidding?" I said to myself and Rusty looked up, wondering if he'd been caught for tearing another Met off the wall.

The only section I actually cared about today? Alright, I'd have to old-school it and just buy one on the way; I'd take Rusty for a quick walk, then we would fire up the VW, and head to Washington DC. Maybe swing by the Exorcist Stairs for old times' sake, say a prayer or something. Couldn't hurt, right?

So, after a quick cup of coffee, I took the world's most energetic dog for a twenty-minute walk. Thankfully, the only hijinks were when a squirrel ran in front of us, and Rusty went nuts and dragged me ten feet into some woods trying to get him. I had no idea what these dog leashes were made of, but the one I got for him could probably be used to tow cars. Anyway, we finished the walk unscathed and I got the basement prepped/barricaded so the pup was good to go, as was I.

Getting in the VW, I started it, heard it chirp to life, and was quickly reminded how much I missed my growling Mustang. I backed the puttering Bug down my driveway and headed for the newsstand a short way down Algonquian where there was a 7-11.

Inside, after a quick "morning!" I headed to the papers, picked one up, and flipped through it to make sure it had a Style section. "Hmph; that's funny, this one doesn't have one either!" I'd just check the next one. There were like ten of them and, by some weird coincidence, well, none of them had it. All ten of them were missing the Style section.

Great; What are the odds of that? I slammed the car door harder than usual and sent my should-be Mustang rocking while I wondered if this was part of a new curse. Luckily, there was a gas station down the street, so I'd just swing by and get one there. And what did I find at Exxon? The same thing. Fourteen papers and none of them had the Style Section. What were the odds? With this week, I'd say pretty good.

I wanted to talk to Madame Pearl and maybe this was a sign that she wanted to speak with me! Yes. That was it. It must have been. Forget the paper, I couldn't change whatever was in there anyway. And I was already headed into DC. Heading down to DC after 10 AM was good for a few reasons: one, all the roads leading to DC were "HOV" (high occupancy, meaning multiple passengers) until 9 AM, so it was easier later, and two, there was *way* less traffic. It was an easy ride, with little traffic, and now I was wishing I had that Hemi under the hood so I could get a little speed in my life. Damn bug was chugging along with Honda's and Toyota's passing me like rockets. *Hah. Ugh. I wish I hadn't mouthed off to a wizard…*

Crossing over the Key Bridge, I made a right onto M Street (I didn't have time for the Exorcist stairs today, besides I'd lived "the Exorcist" that week) and headed down to Madame Pearl's shop. As I pulled in front, I noticed a sign said "closed." Just as I thought, but I was hoping to still see her, so I parked and walked around the back to where she might park, or go in, and saw no cars anywhere. I looked at the upstairs windows, and they were all dark. It looked like she wasn't in.

Damn! All I wanted was to talk to her, and just apologize. I know I was rude to her, and really just wanted to let her know that. I knew if this spell was really happening, I probably didn't deserve a pass for the last day and wasn't even going to ask for one. And since it looked like she was not there, I wouldn't even have a chance to. Just as I was about to give up, I realized I'd seen a notepad in the glove box in my Bug, which, incidentally, wouldn't have been there if I still had my car; I decided to just jot down a quick note and leave it in her door. Assuming I survived whatever may or may not happen today, I'd come back and be sure to give an in person, full-hearted apology.

Dear Madame Pearl,

I am extremely sorry for insulting you, your industry, or Palm Readers anywhere, and meant no harm. I don't know if you had anything to do with any of the wacky events that happened to me this week, and were eerily like my horoscopes, but, if you did, I don't blame you on account of my rudeness. If you did have anything to do with them, I want to thank you; I met someone in New Jersey, that I need to see again. My car may have caught on fire, exploded, and is now burnt, but despite all that, I am going to go back and finish my chat with her. If I can find her. I'm hopeful my car cooperates with things this time.

Anyway, I wanted to tell you this in person, and hope to see you sometime soon, but if I don't see you please know I'm sorry and wish you all the best.

I signed the letter and folded it up neatly before heading up the stairs that led to her second-floor entrance. I figured I'd put it through the mailbox slot then head back to NYC as the boss ordered.

When I reached the top of the stairs, I heard:

"She's not there, young man. Madame Pearl was rushed to the hospital late yesterday, and we haven't heard from her or family. I tried to call the hospital for news, but they wouldn't give me anything over the phone."

I turned toward the voice but didn't see anyone.

"What?"

"That's right, she was rushed yesterday afternoon to GW Hospital cross town. She was not looking good. She was on a stretcher and they sped out of here. Like I said, I tried calling the hospital, but they wouldn't give me any news. I've known her for years, my shop's been next to hers all this time, and they wouldn't tell me anything. Apparently, she'd been feeling ill all week."

"Oh, no. That's such sad news. Her granddaughter told me she had the flu. Do you think it's related to that? I'm going to go up there and see if I can find anything out." It felt odd talking to a voice I couldn't see but given this week anything could have happened and I would have taken it in stride.

I turned a few circles looking for the source of the voice when the door to the souvenir shop next door cracked open and another cute old lady peaked out. The lady next door shook her head and held out her hand from her doorway. I took it and she wished me well and asked me to let the family know she was sending her prayers.

I jumped in the car and nervously called Marissa's cell phone and got her voice mail. I left a message letting her know I heard about her grandmother and to please call me. And no, I didn't care about the horoscopes anymore, I just wanted to find out how she's doing and to please call me.

Why was it whenever you needed to be somewhere quickly, it was always then when traffic was the worst? I pulled out onto M Street in DC, and as soon as I did, got stuck behind a trash truck going 15 mph and stopping every ten feet.

"Hey buddy, can you please pull way over to the right so I can get around you? I'm in a hurry."

"So is everybody else, guy. Unfortunately for you, everybody else also has a lot of trash to pick up. On Fridays. Like today."

"C'mon man, I need to get to GW Hospital; a friend of mine's there."

I didn't know if he could hear me, or was flat out ignoring me, but this was nuts. I considered going far left, and dodging oncoming traffic, but that was no good. Everything was locked up. Except the sidewalk. Which I looked at, very closely, then checked for cops (none), and did what I do best: improvise. Right over the curb, thru some trash (sorry boys, maybe you should've let me pass), and hauled ass down the sidewalk, very carefully I might add.

About thirty feet down I jumped back onto M Street and rubbed the dash of my gorgeous, tricky little car. If my car hadn't blown up, I'd have had the Mustang and there's no way I could have taken that machine up on the sidewalk. Was there any valuable customer feedback for my maneuver? Only if you counted a fruit vendor gunning an orange down the sidewalk at me. I also might have caught one of the garbage men flipping me off. A deserved response. Good thing these were rental plates.

The drivers on the opposite side of the road were watching my little detour with mouths agape and I actually got them fired up because they immediately started honking to get traffic moving again. If I didn't know better, I would've thought I was back in New Jersey, driving like a maniac with a tail of flames in my wake.

I pulled up in front of GW, parked right off to the side of the emergency entrance, and ran to the front desk.

"Hello, a good friend of mine was brought in here last night and we haven't heard any news. Can you please help me?"

"Sure, what's your friend's name?"

It was then I realized I have no idea what her name really was. I decided to take a long shot.

"Mrs. Pearl. She's the grandmother of a dear, dear friend of mine," who, apparently, was not speaking to me, I realized as I checked my phone again—a fact I kept to myself. "She hasn't been well all week and she was brought in last night. Please, I just want to know if she's ok."

"Are you family?"

I flashed quickly to my sidewalk venture and knew I had to improvise again. "She's the grandmother of my fiancé! Please. All I want to know is if she's ok, maybe a quick visit."

"OK, she's on the 5th floor, room 512; go on up."

I thanked the nurse and bolted to the elevator. On the fifth floor I headed to the 500 block following signs and arrows pointing the way. Rooms 502, 504, and 508 all had people in them. I passed two more rooms, both teaming with people, before I found 512, with the number 1 in the sequence missing—and it was empty!

"Hello, can I help you?" A helpful nurse was at my back.

"Yes, I'm looking for Mrs. Pearl, she was in here."

"I'm so sorry..." then at that same time an alarm went off.

"Oh no! That's a code blue emergency! I need to go!" And she literally ran out of the room.

"Oh no" was right. I was staring at this vacant room and had just been told "I'm so sorry" by a nurse; I didn't know what to think. I looked outside the room into the hall and there was a lot of commotion—people running down the corridor to apparently work on whatever a "code blue" was. I hoped they were OK, whoever was in trouble. Even the person at the desk was busy; she was calling for a Dr. Wilson on the loudspeakers, so was of no help to me.

I needed to know what happened to Madame Pearl; I was still by her room, so went back in. In the excitement, I dropped my letter to her, I realized, and went to get it by the foot of the severely empty bed. That's when I noticed a package on the seat in the corner of her room. Returning my letter to my pocket, I went over and grabbed the package. Inside the well-wrapped box was an envelope with my name on it (*ok, how in the world did she know my name!?*), a small bag, and underneath it, a copy of today's Washington Post!

I quickly opened the envelope and found a letter, handwritten in sweet, grandma scribble that reminded me of birthday cards I received when I was a kid. I braced myself as I started to read: (I almost didn't want to, but of course needed to).

> My dear young Billy,
> I trust you've had an entertaining week! And I hope it wasn't too exciting, or painful, but, young man, I am hopeful a valuable lesson has been learned. No, I do not think you are the Devil, and without redemptive hope. Had I thought that, perhaps the week would've been a bit more lively than I trust it was.

No, I saw, deep down, you're a considerate young man, who, I believe, if given an opportunity, would re-think your actions, and come around; you just needed a little nudge. I decided to give it to you. My intent was not to punish you, but to enlighten you; I hope I did.

With that being said: try not to judge others too quickly. I've included a little poem for you, which may prove helpful for you to remember that from time to time. It's below:

Sometimes we're mean during this lifelong dance,
But you're not so undeserving, of a real second chance,
With that being said, carry this till the end,
Take a trip, take a chance, and make a new friend.
And remember, please be nice.
Now don't be a stranger! I hope you like the present in the bag and come see me some time.

Grandma Pearl

I was stunned. *What a sweet note, and the bag?* It had three giant chocolate chip cookies, just like the ones she gave Marissa the night when this debacle started. And since there was a Washington Post here, I had to check the Style Section, and maybe I could see my horoscope. I turned to the correct page and read:

LEO
"Sometimes we're mean during this lifelong dance,
But you're not so undeserving, of a real second chance,
With that being said, carry this till the end,
Take a trip, take a chance, and make a new friend
And remember, please be nice."

Wow! I couldn't believe it even though I saw it there in front of my eyes. And no one else would ever believe me if I told them—maybe not even Mike. But I knew the truth, and yes, maybe I had learned something. Her letter matched the horoscope word for word. That was some serious mojo. Not only was I grateful, but I was even more upset. I didn't know if she was ok or not, and I was incredibly rude to her the last time I saw her. I needed to find out how she was doing. I hoped she's ok, but I still need to know.

Just then I heard a voice.

"Well? Did you learn anything?"

It was Madame Pearl, along with Marissa, and a very large guy who I could only assume was the brother that wanted to talk to Mike.

I quickly looked away to get myself composed. (I thought she was telling fortunes in the Great Beyond and was starting to choke up). I cleared my throat.

"Of course! And I'm glad you're OK. Are you OK?"

"Yes, I just had a touch of the flu and passed out. I believe it was from a cheeseburger from a restaurant that shall remain unmanned (she was looking menacingly at Marissa), but I'm ok. Now the question still stands, have the events of the past week taught you anything?"

"Yes! It did. I have a whole new respect and appreciation for palm reading, horoscopes, fortune telling...all of it!"

"Young man, I'm relieved of that, but is that all you learned? I was hoping for something else. Perhaps you should read the note again. I was hoping for something with a little more depth. And no, *not* the poem."

"Do you mean the part about judging others? Like maybe I shouldn't be so quick to?"

"No, I meant the part about you not being the Devil..." she paused for dramatic effect, I realized after my heart sank to my feet and the others did all they could to not laugh, "...*Of course* I meant the part about judging others; you see, I'm an old lady and seen more than my share of that over the years. Do yourself a favor and don't be so quick to judge what you don't understand. It's not fair to them, or you, and it's just not nice. There is too much meanness in the world today. Don't add to it! Bring the positive into the discussion. Not the meanness. Now c'mere and give me a hug and go do something nice before I turn you into a frog. *Just kidding*, that one never works!! Maybe you'll come visit the shop from time to time and pay an old lady a visit. Perhaps get a palm reading if you're brave enough. Marissa, honey, please get my coat. We're leaving."

That was why they had come back; her coat was in the closet! And just then the nurse returned.

"Ohhhh, I'm so glad you found each other. This young man was very worried about you."

"I know. We've caught up on everything, and I have a feeling we'll be seeing more of him in the future. I'm good with that sort of thing."

Of course she was. And of course I hugged her and said goodbye. And I would be sure to visit Grandma Pearl once in awhile, maybe see if she needed something heavy moved, or something fixed, or maybe just to say hello and see how she's doing. I had a hard-learned respect for her and, if I was being honest, a bit of fear about what she could put me through!

She and Marissa headed to the nurse's station to check out, and I headed to the stairs.

"And tell your friend Mike to come by the restaurant if he wants to apologize, too! I might be in a better mood this time. Just tell him not to bring Rex, or whatever that beast's name is. I like smaller dogs. I also can't wait to see his race car!"

"Ok I will, and it was nice to see you again!"

I had to admit I chuckled at the thought of Rusty and his chaos. That dog was as consistent as my posse: always making new friends. Either on golf courses, fancy restaurants, or dog parks. And Mike? Consistent to the very end. I'd let him deal with the "race car" white lie.

As I started down the stairs to get to my car, I received two text messages, one from Mike, and another from Ray in New Jersey. I checked Mike's first.

"Billy, quick call me. You're not going to believe this, but my horoscope said something about me being fed a meal fit for a King, and later that day, a truck swerved hard around a corner to avoid a car and dumped it's cargo on me. It's food cargo. OF HAMBURGERS. BURGER KING HAMBURGERS!!! Help! I'm sorry I didn't believe you!"

I had to chuckle as I responded, "Were they cooked the way you like 'em? That's what Burger King supposedly does! I can't help you now, I have to go back to New York! I suggest you lay low, be nice, and maybe you call Marissa and beg for help. And no, you can't borrow Rusty. Or my car. Good luck, see you in a week."

Then, onto text number two—this one from Ray:

"Billy, give me a call, your car is ready, and something else. --Ray"

I quickly dialed him. "Hey Ray, how are you, and my car is ready?"

"Yes, and more; ten minutes ago, a blonde in a black Dodge Charger was here looking for a taillight, saying something about 'if that guy hadn't sped off, I would have talked to him. I have no idea what happened to him or his Mustang.'

"I told her to come back tomorrow, and I'd have the taillight. She said she'll be back around 3 PM then. I think it might be a good idea if you were here, picking up your parts around then, too."

Unreal. Grandma Pearl was helping me after all that! And Ray, too. Well, I quickly put in a call to my dog walkers, arranged for them to watch Rusty overnight, gassed up the VW, and started my drive back to New Jersey, then, of course, to New York to finish the Statue job, and hopefully rescue my career.

***

SATURDAY
Epilogue

I sped up 95 North till I saw the exit to Ray's repair shop in Bordentown. When I pulled up, I saw two black vehicles in front. One of which was a really cool looking Dodge Charger, with a broken left taillight, and another vehicle, a 1973 Ford Mustang, with a very rough look.

Just then Ray came out.

"Billy! Am I glad to see you. We had some trouble locating that rear spring and shock, but we've got 'em. Let me tell you what's going on with it." He slapped me on the back and guided me toward the cars and must have felt my apprehension.

"No, no. It's running great now, though the back floor is gone, the back window on the fastback part is 90% gone, and the interior back is torched. But the drive train is not damaged, and I installed a new gas tank, and all connections."

"Is it safe? I mean with all that exposed, this thing isn't gonna blow up on me while I drive it home, is it?"

"No, not at all. It looks like it's been through a war zone, but it's running fine, and the taillights are even working now. That 429 engine you have in it is a gem."

"Boy, this does look rough. Don't I need a back window? and the paint is torched..."

A more scientific look was that the paint, which was once shiny black from the front till the back wheels, was now sporting a charring worthy of an exploded laboratory. What was left was flat black with much of it burnt off exposing the grey (and charred) steel on the back half of the car. Looking inside, I found the front to be ok (including the bucket seats), but the back seat was totally gone, the headliner burnt and shredded, and most of the back floor gone, exposing the stuff underneath it. You know, a shiny new gas tank, the drive shaft, and you could even see the back wheels.

"Are you sure this thing is safe to drive?" I repeated, not quite ready to experience another near-fatal crash.

"Yes, my mechanic, Pete, the one over there, took it out and wants to buy it. Something about using it for drag races, or Halloween as a Batmobile gone bad. Anyway, he took it out on the Turnpike an hour ago and ran it hard. It looks rough, but it ran great.

"How about I take it, and come back in a day or so? I need to get back home. Also, would you please turn in this VW to Enterprise for me? I really need to get rolling."

"The flower-mobile? Christ. None of my guys are gonna drive that thing. I'll have to do it."

Just then, a smoking hot blonde came out of the shop.

"Ray, thanks very much for the taillight. Ohhh. Whose VW Bug is that?!"

I was about to duck and pretend it had nothing to do with me when out of her mouth came a squeal and, "I love it!"

"Well, it's mine. Sort of. I'm renting it while I pick up my Mustang over there."

"Oh, wait a minute, I know you! You nearly killed me and broke my taillight. Also, that fire thing!"

After a quick set of introductions from Ray, I found out that Annie, was a huge car fan, and actually dug my car and wanted to talk to me all about it. Also, that her kid sister was looking for a VW bug with flowers all over it, like a 60s hippie car. Clearly the stars were aligning, and I made a silent prayer again thanking Grandma Pearl.

"If you like, Annie, I bet the owner of this may want to sell it. I have to go to NY for a quick project, then could help you negotiate with him."

"Would you?"

"Of course, but if I do, you have to promise to have dinner with me in New York. And I guarantee where we have dinner is the best view in all of New York City."

"Ok, but where?"

"I guarantee you'll like it, and I also guarantee your friends will be jealous."

Annie gave me a sly look and shook her head. For a moment my heart sank, but she converted the disapproval to a smile and a shy but firm, "Yes."

And so it went, four hours later, we ate some of the greatest Chinese food ever, on a small box in the torch of the Statue of Liberty, witnessing the most glorious sunset I had ever seen. In the coolest spot as well.

"Do you really work here?" Annie asked as she was pulling a lo mein noodle out of our takeout cartons using chopsticks like a pro. "I think the Statue of Liberty is the best monument of them all!"

"I don't work here, but I get to come up here from time to time. And I like it too but am not sure it's the best of them all, I'll have to think about that. A good friend of mine recently suggested to me to slow down and not judge things too quickly and I'm trying to, particularly the quick judging. More tea, my dear?"

I chuckled to myself over this, if only Madame Pearl could see me now.

Annie put her meal to the side, looked me over with her hands at her sides, and then leaned in for a kiss on the cheek. At the same time, the torch lit up; I don't know what was brighter, the torch or me blushing. I'm sure it was the torch, I'm way too cool to blush. At least that's my story and I'm sticking to it.

And so ended my week. And what a week it was. I wouldn't have believed it if I didn't live it. Looking back, I wouldn't have changed a thing, even if I could.

***

ABOUT THE AUTHOR

Stuart McCusker lives in Northern Virginia in a suburb of Washington, DC and works for a Fortune 500 company. He has two great kids, a crazy dog (a boxer named Rusty), and is a huge NY Mets fan. This is his first book, and he hopes you enjoy it very much. He is working on two others and hopes to have them out in 2020.

Made in the USA
Middletown, DE
26 April 2020

91756456R00092